Pilfering the Pink Pearls

A Witch's Cove Mystery
Book 15

Vella Day

Pilfering the Pink Pearls
Copyright © 2021 by Vella Day
Print Edition
www.velladay.com
velladayauthor@gmail.com

Cover Art by Jaycee DeLorenzo
Edited by Rebecca Cartee

Published in the United States of America
Print book ISBN: 978-1-951430-39-9

ALL RIGHTS RESERVED. No part of this book may be used or reproduced in any manner whatsoever without written permission of the author except in the case of brief questions embodied in critical articles or reviews.

This is a work of fiction. Names, characters, places, and incidents either are the product of the author's imagination or are used fictitiously, and any resemblance to actual persons living or dead, business establishments, events or locales, is entirely coincidental.

How far would you go not to age? Would you commit murder? Well, someone decided to.

Welcome to Witch's Cove, where the strangest of cases occur. Murder often abounds, but so does time travel, shifters, and evil warlocks.

When the elegant Alexandria Coronado asks for my help in finding her pink pearl necklace that was stolen from the Magic Wand Hotel, I had no idea it would involve murder, scuba diving, and a massive empire. Because our sheriff suspects magic is involved, he is willing to join forces with the Pink Iguana sleuths. That's where I come in. Hi, I'm Glinda Goodall, and I'm a witch, who together with my fiancé, run our sleuth business.

At first, I thought this was going to be another run-of-the-mill theft case, but when Alexandria goes scuba diving and is lost at sea, it turns into a lot more. Finding that she is a super wealthy heiress of a vitamin empire, makes our suspect list grow even more.

If you want to be kept up-to-date on where we are in solving this case, stop by our office, or just look upward to find a black wing-tipped seagull. Where he is, you might find Iggy, my talking pink iguana, who is always in the know.

Chapter One

"I WANT TO report a crime. Someone *stole* my pink pearl necklace, which was *locked* in my hotel room's safe." The woman's voice grew louder with each word.

That irate guest was in the lobby of the Magic Wand Hotel, and her voice was close to a shout. Since the front desk was just out of sight of the hotel restaurant where Jaxson Harrison and I were having dinner to celebrate our one month engagement, we could hear her quite clearly. Naturally, I wanted to see who was making this allegation, but that would be rude. Why? Because I wanted this dinner to be about us—not our job.

In case you're wondering why I would care, I'm Glinda Goodall, half owner of The Pink Iguana Sleuths agency. Whenever I hear of a potential crime, my ears perk up.

I turned to my business partner and fiancé. "I can't remember hearing about any thefts in this hotel before. Have you?"

"No. Ted and Nate run a tight ship. You planning to find out what's going on?" His cute little smirk implied he knew I wanted to.

"No. This is our time." I held up my glass of wine and tapped it against his beer bottle, proud that I wanted to put our date above my curiosity.

"I greatly appreciate the gesture, but I have the sense I won't have your full attention until you get a visual on this woman. Go ahead. When you return, you can tell me all about it." Jaxson leaned back in his chair and held up his beer.

I could argue, but he'd insist—or at least I hope he would. "You know me too well."

He grinned. "I do. Now go."

I almost giggled, which probably wasn't all that classy for a twenty-eight-year old. Regardless, I pushed back my chair and headed out to the lobby. I wanted to look like I was a guest and not someone merely interested in the drama unfolding at the reception desk. Too bad I was never great at the cloak and dagger stuff.

All I needed was a peek, so I shot a quick glance in her direction. A moderately good-looking gentleman and a tall, attractive woman were standing at the front desk. The man didn't appear all that interested in what the lady was saying since he was studying the rack of keys behind the clerk instead of paying attention to the complaint.

The female guest was a different matter. She was leaning over the desk, her palms planted on the surface. Her dark hair was pulled back in a ponytail, and except for the large, teardrop diamond earrings, I might have thought she was about to go for a run. The tight black pants were topped with a fitted, light blue sleeveless shirt that looked like something one would see on the cover of a fitness magazine—not that I looked at many of those. Working out wasn't my thing.

The forty-something-year old woman had both muscles and beauty and appeared to be the one in charge since the man wasn't saying anything. The man, on the other hand, was dressed in a pair of dark charcoal gray pants and a white button-down shirt. I'd put him a good fifteen years older than the woman.

"What are you going to do about this travesty?" The owner of the necklace asked, clearly incensed. She didn't seem to have a problem taking out her anger on the poor employee either.

I wasn't impressed with her rather rude—or maybe I should say desperate—approach, but if the necklace was as valuable as she made it out to be, I might be upset too. If someone took my grandmother's magical pink pendant, I'd be a total basket case, and I might even be raising my voice. A lot.

The man looked up and lasered me with a stare. Whoops. Caught. Having no desire for him to come over and question me, I walked over to one of the side tables next to the hotel's seating area, picked up a random fishing magazine, and flipped through the pages, pretending as if I was totally fascinated with it. I hoped he believed I was just a guest wanting to know the ins and outs of tarpon fishing.

The man must have told the woman she was making a scene because she lowered her voice, and my ability to snoop dropped close to zero.

While Jaxson and I didn't eat here often, the same two or three clerks always worked the reception desk. Unfortunately, tonight, a new employee was there, which made extracting any gossip less than certain. I felt sorry for the young girl, but she seemed to be handling the verbal abuse as well as could be expected.

After a proper amount of time, I turned around and returned to the restaurant, making sure not to glance their way.

"Well?" Jaxson asked as soon as I sat down.

I told him my impression of the woman. "I just hope they can find the thief."

"What are you going to do about it?"

That brought a smile to my lips. "Who says I'm going to do anything?"

"Glinda Goodall. You wouldn't be you if you didn't want to know what happened and then try to help."

"True, but this seems to be something for our sheriff's department to handle."

"Uh-huh."

"Fine. I'll ask our gossip queens tomorrow what they know, but for tonight, I want this dinner to be about us."

Jaxson tilted his head. "What's going on? Your romantic side is showing." He smiled. "I have to say, I like it."

"Funny man." I wanted to change the subject—or rather needed to. "On a different note, I'm worried about Iggy."

Iggy is my familiar who is a pink iguana—and yes, I am a witch. I still suffer some guilt over the fact that my spell turned him from green to pink. To this day, Iggy is a bit sensitive about his color, not that I can blame him. At least my familiar can talk and do a lot of other things that no ordinary iguana can.

Jaxson sat up straighter. "Why are you worried? He seems fine to me, other than he's on constant alert for his nemesis, Tippy."

Tippy was this rather distinctive seagull with black-tipped

wings who seemed determined to harass my familiar—or so Iggy claimed. "For the last two weeks, he's been sleeping under the hibiscus tree by the office to make sure the seagulls don't eat the flowers."

"But he's sleeping, right?"

"I guess. It's warm this time of year, but what happens when winter comes?" Florida has been known to have a freeze or two. That kind of weather would kill Iggy.

"I'll talk with him. How is his petition to ban all seagulls from the beach coming?" Jaxson swallowed a smile.

We both knew that was a joke, but we all humored Iggy. Ever since the seagull leader—Tippy—pooped on him a time or two, my poor sixteen-year-old iguana couldn't focus on anything but getting his revenge. That was a tall mountain to climb since Iggy couldn't fly.

When my cousin, Rihanna, my Aunt Fern, and our witch friend Andorra helped collect signatures to present to the mayor, everyone thought it was cute. And yes, they recognized it for what it was—something to appease the agitated iguana.

"The mayor will put Iggy off for as long as he can, but at some point Iggy will catch on that nothing can be done about his problem," I said.

The most bizarre thing about this petition was that the mayor didn't really believe Iggy could talk. Why? Because only witches, warlocks, and some other special people could communicate with him. And the mayor was only a human.

"I bet if we offer our services to this woman to help find her necklace, Iggy will want to be involved. He's always more energized when we have a case."

Jaxson had a point. "True, but let's see what the sheriff

comes up with first." We often ended up being involved in Steve Rocker's cases anyway, especially if there was an element of magic. "If we knew the occult was somehow a part of this, I'd offer our assistance right away."

"Sounds like a plan."

Not really, but I was determined not to dwell on it any more tonight. I wanted to celebrate being with Jaxson.

I waited until after we finished our meal before I suggested we speak with the desk clerk to get the scoop on this woman's complaint. Unfortunately, the shift had changed. Darn. Tomorrow, I was determined to find out more.

THE NEXT MORNING, I awoke to bright light streaming in through my bedroom window, which meant I'd overslept. I usually sleep in late, but this was late even for me. I realized we didn't have a case, but since my nineteen-year-old cousin, Rihanna, was attending classes at the nearby community college, Jaxson would be at the office by himself—assuming he decided to go into work today. If we were without a case, he often would wander downstairs to his brother's wine and cheese shop to help out.

I whipped off my covers, dressed, and got ready to face the day. "Iggy?" I called out as I went into the living room.

No answer. I looked around but didn't see him. I then checked the kitchen. My one-bedroom apartment only had three rooms—or more like two and a half since the kitchen was kind of an extension of the living room. Where was my familiar?

Considering it was later than usual, he either was visiting his girlfriend, Aimee, who was the talking cat that lived with my Aunt Fern across the hallway, or he'd already waddled over to the office. As much as he would have liked to be at the Hex and Bones Apothecary visiting Hugo, one of our resident gargoyle shifters, Iggy knew that crossing a busy street was dangerous. Being less than four-inches tall, it was difficult to see him even though he was pink.

Since my iguana could take care of himself for the most part, I walked to the office, which was a mere two buildings away. When I arrived, Jaxson was at his computer. Good.

I leaned over and kissed his cheek. "Good morning, or should I say good afternoon?"

He swiveled around in his chair and grinned. "You slept well, I take it?"

"I did. I'm sorry I'm late, but I kind of conked out after our wonderful dinner date last night."

He smiled. "I did too."

As much as I wanted to rehash the part of the evening that had been romantic, I still wasn't comfortable talking about intense emotions despite being engaged to him.

I refocused on something less personal. On his computer screen sat a weather map. "What are you working on?"

"I heard about a hurricane forming in the Atlantic."

I hissed in a breath and leaned closer. Hurricanes were always scary for Floridians. Thankfully, since we lived on the west side of Florida, we didn't get as many as the east coast did. "That's not good."

"No, and while we haven't had a category 4 or 5 directly hit in my lifetime, we can get high winds that can do a lot of damage."

"I know. When is the next one expected to arrive?"

"She's called tropical storm Irma, and she might not even come up the Gulf. If she does though, she won't be here for another two days."

"Good. We need to make sure that Aunt Fern has the boards ready to batten down the hatches if the storm heads this way."

He nodded. "I'll help."

"That would be great."

Jaxson looked around. "Where's Iggy? He didn't come with you?"

"No. He wasn't at the apartment when I got up either. I thought he might be here. Since he's not, he's probably visiting Aimee. I should have checked, but I hadn't had my morning coffee or any breakfast—or should I say, lunch—yet."

He leaned back and smiled. "Would you like to grab some food now?"

"I do like a man who can read my mind. How about the diner?" I was certain Iggy would be fine. He might even be out and about looking for Tippy.

"You got it. I'm assuming you plan to find out if Dolly knows anything about the pearl necklace heist at the hotel last night?"

"Of course, I am. I figure by now, Steve will have already investigated, which means information should have already spread by now." The gossip queen chain was very strong in Witch's Cove.

We were amateur sleuths—who occasionally were paid—

and as such, we were experts at knowing the right people to talk with. Dolly Andrews, the owner of the Spellbound Diner, was one such person, and she was always willing to impart and receive gossip. Since she was good friends with Pearl Dillsmith, the sheriff's grandmother and receptionist, we received a lot of good info from her.

Jaxson pushed back his chair. "I have to say I'm surprised Iggy isn't here. You did tell him about the heist last night, didn't you?"

"No, he was asleep when I got home."

"I'm sure he's heard about it by now, which means he'll be back to get the details."

"I imagine he will," I said.

I thought about leaving a note telling him where we would be—and yes, he can read—but I didn't need him prancing into the diner. Despite wearing a collar, visitors might freak if they spotted a lizard in an eating establishment.

Jaxson and I headed down the stairs. At the bottom, I scanned all of the freshly planted hibiscus bushes to see if any animals had attacked the plants—plants that served as Iggy's favorite food. What I didn't expect was to see my familiar asleep under one of the bushes. I tapped Jaxson's shoulder.

He nodded. "I should have known."

"Me, too. He probably got up early and came over here to finish his nap, thinking his mere presence would deter the seagulls. For all I know, it does. Let's leave him be." We remained quiet as we headed to the diner, which was a short walk down the main street.

Every time I stepped into Dolly's old-fashioned establishment, it took me back to my childhood where I would sit at the counter with my parents or grandmother, drinking a chocolate shake. I remember Dolly always had a smile on her face. Her father had started the diner, and she'd picked up where he left off.

When we entered, I waved to her, and she came around the counter to greet us, like she did most of her guests.

"Hey, you guys. Let me see it," Dolly said.

I had no idea what she was talking about. "See what?"

She rolled her eyes. "Your engagement ring."

I couldn't believe I hadn't shown it to her before. I'd had the ring a month, but part of the time, the ring had been at the jewelers being sized. "Oh, this old thing?" I chuckled. "It was Jaxson's grandmother's ring. Isn't it gorgeous?" I wiggled the fingers on my ring hand.

"Totally. I couldn't be happier for you guys."

"Thanks, Dolly."

"Have a seat anywhere, and I'll be over to take your order."

I was hoping she would do more than just provide us with food. Gossip was my game today.

We sat in our usual booth. "I'm surprised she didn't mention the theft. Surely, Pearl would have told her about it." Nothing got by Pearl—or almost nothing.

"Maybe she thinks we already know what happened at the hotel last night and plans to pick our brains," he said.

"It wouldn't be the first time, and yes, I know, gossip is a two-way street."

A few minutes later, Dolly returned. "Sorry about that. I bet you've heard about that poor woman at the Magic Wand Hotel who had her necklace stolen last night."

I nodded. "We have, but I don't know much. Do you have the scoop?"

"Not really. Pearl said that the woman who was robbed was some rich heiress from Atlanta who runs a vitamin company. I think Pearl did a little research and found the woman was some distant relative to the Coca-Cola fortune."

No wonder she was rich—assuming she inherited any family money. I had to chuckle. "And here you didn't think you knew much."

She smiled. "I meant, I wish I knew more."

I looked over at Jaxson. "It's more than I know. My only contribution is that I saw her at the front desk when she told the clerk that someone had taken her pearl necklace from her locked safe."

Dolly acted as if she'd learned that too. "She's supposed to be some fitness guru. Is she stunning?"

"Totally. She is tall, thin, and fit. And yes, beautiful."

Dolly sighed. "It's unfair for one person to be rich and good looking."

I glanced over at Jaxson and sighed. "I'm rich since I have a wonderful man in my life." I reached out and clasped his hand.

"That's twice in a twenty-four hour period that you've been romantic," he said.

He was right about that. Jaxson was usually the one to talk more about love than I was. "You bring it out in me."

"Okay, you two." Dolly sounded a little embarrassed. "Promise you'll let me know if you learn anything?"

"Of course. Pearl didn't tell you anything else?"

She tapped her pencil on her pad. "Not much other than

Steve and Nash are on the case. It is a theft, so they have to investigate."

"If someone stole this woman's necklace from the hotel safe, it could be long gone by now."

Dolly nodded. "Sad but true."

By the time we finished ordering, I'd made up my mind. I wanted to help this lady find what was rightfully hers.

Chapter Two

"YOU REALLY THINK that Pearl knows more than what she told Dolly?" Jaxson asked as we crossed the street to the sheriff's department.

"We're about to find out!" I had to hold my hair back to keep the wind from whipping it around. "I thought the storm wasn't supposed to show up for two more days."

He smiled. "This is just a typical summer squall."

I guess all of his computer research on weather was paying off.

When we entered the office, Pearl looked up, shoved her knitting in the drawer, and smiled. "Hello, you two. It's been a while."

I suppose we hadn't had a case in a bit. "It has been." I hand brushed my messy hair. "So, what can you tell us about the robbery at the hotel last night?"

Her eyes slightly widened. "Did Dolly tell you?"

I didn't want to implicate her, though all of the gossip queens understood that it was their job in life to disseminate information. "Actually, Jaxson and I were at dinner when we overheard that poor woman tell the clerk that someone had stolen her necklace."

"Oh, so you've met Alexandria Coronado?"

"That's her name?" It sounded as elegant as she looked.

"Yes. She and her family are down from Atlanta."

Not that we don't get a lot of tourists, but September was one of our warmest and most humid months, so many vacationers didn't visit then. "I saw her, but I didn't introduce myself. It definitely wasn't the right time. She was a bit preoccupied, shall we say."

"I can understand that."

"Do you know why she's in Witch's Cove?" Usually, rich heiresses didn't pick our small Florida town as a vacation destination.

"No, but maybe she's a witch and wants to connect with her kind." Pearl grinned.

"Could be." A lot of people came to Witch's Cove because of the name. They either wanted to meet a witch, or they were one themselves and wanted to be part of a group.

Steve came out of his office and stopped when he saw us. "Come to pick my grandmother's brain?"

Thank goodness he didn't seem upset, but by now the sheriff should be used to me always snooping. "We're just here to see if we can help in anyway with last night's hotel robbery."

He sobered. "Did you hear magic was involved or something?"

That hadn't crossed my mind—at least not since last night—but I found it curious that he'd ask. "No, did you?"

"Why don't you come on back to my office?"

I knew Steve Rocker well enough to know that he must have suspected magic, or he wouldn't have mention it. Jaxson and I followed him back.

Once seated, we waited for him to tell us what in the world was going on. He usually initiated things, so when he remained quiet, I had to prod him. "So?"

"I'm sure you are aware that it was Alexandria Coronado who was robbed last night."

I didn't want to mention that I'd never heard of her before Pearl told me. "As a matter of fact, Jaxson and I were having dinner at the Magic Wand and heard Mrs. Coronado express her displeasure."

He huffed out a laugh. "According to the clerk, that would be an understatement."

"Let's say that if someone had stolen my necklace, I'd have freaked out, too."

"Yes, but your necklace is magic. I never have asked you before, but if someone borrowed your necklace, could they use it to detect how a person died, like you can?"

"I've never lent it to anyone so I don't know, and my grandmother never said if it would work for anyone else. If it did, he or she would have to be a warlock or a witch."

"Do you think Rihanna could use it successfully?"

"Maybe." Rihanna was my cousin, and she was a witch. "I should ask her to give it a try sometime. Why are you asking? Did Mrs. Coronado say she was a witch?"

"No, but she didn't deny it either."

Something must have led him to believe that she was one. "I trust you've checked all of the hotel rooms for this necklace?"

"Of course. I even called in Misty and her crew to help search."

Misty was the sheriff over in Liberty. She was also Steve's

girlfriend. "You looked in every safe and found nothing, right?"

"Glinda, I know how to do my job."

I'd pushed a little too hard. "Sorry. I can't help it. None of the family members or staff knew anything, I take it?"

His smile was brief. "No."

"What's your next step?"

His brows rose. "Me? I was hoping you'd offer to do a locator spell."

Never in a million years did I expect our sheriff, who possessed no warlock abilities, to suggest that.

I looked over at Jaxson, who seemed to understand how misguided our sheriff was.

"Glinda isn't connected to Mrs. Coronado's necklace, and she needs to be somehow in order for the spell to work," Jaxson explained.

"You found Rihanna when she went missing." He wagged a finger. "Oh, yeah she's a relative."

"Yes. Having someone close to the missing item is a must."

"How about if we ask Mrs. Coronado to help? It's her necklace," Steve said.

"Sure, but she needs to be a witch." There were some workarounds, but I wasn't sure if even Gertrude Poole, our most powerful psychic, could pull it off.

"I see. What do you suggest?"

I had to think about that. "I guess I could check out her room to see if I get a vibe off of the safe. That might help." I waited to see if he'd buy it. I've never gotten a vibe off of anything, but there was always a first time. To be honest, I just wanted to look around the room—and meet her. "Or I could ask Genevieve to join me."

Genevieve Dubois was a gargoyle shifter who had many talents. I wasn't convinced even she was aware of all of her abilities since she'd only been in her human form a short while—long story.

Steve seemed to think about that. "How about you see what you can do first. If that fails, we can call in the big guns."

That meant asking Genevieve, Hugo, or maybe Gertrude Poole. "Okay, but I'd like Iggy to help."

His eyebrows rose. "Because?"

"For starters, his sense of smell is better than anyone's." I held up my hand. "I realize we have a few werewolves in our midst, but Iggy has other talents."

"Such as?"

"If he explores the safe, he might be able to detect something unusual."

Steve tapped his pen against his yellow note pad. "Works for me."

Jaxson placed a hand on my shoulder. "I'll get him, assuming he's where we last saw him."

"Thanks."

While we waited for Jaxson to return with Iggy, Steve called Alexandria Coronado and explained that a witch with special powers wanted to give the search a try. What? Steve actually believed I have special powers? What was he thinking? My familiar had the ability to see and smell things, but I did not. I hope this woman didn't expect a miracle, because I'd been fresh out of them as of late.

Steve nodded. "Okay. Yes, I'll be with her and her fiancé."

He disconnected. "All set."

"Was she hesitant or excited?" I wasn't sure if it would make a difference, but I liked to understand her frame of mind.

"I would say relieved that I was bringing in someone with the potential to help. Bottom line is that she just wants her necklace back."

"I don't blame her. I hope I don't disappoint her. If Alexandria admits that she is a witch, then a locator spell might be in order."

"Let's take it one step at a time."

Jaxson returned a few minutes later, carrying a sleepy iguana. "Hey, buddy, time to wake up."

Iggy cracked open an eye. "You rang?"

Sometimes Iggy could be so silly. "You can't still be tired. You were sleeping when we spotted you." I lifted him out of Jaxson's hands.

Iggy lifted his head. "I'm good. I just needed a moment. Jaxson said you could use my expertise?"

"Yes."

"Will Hugo be there?" Poor thing loved spending time with his gargoyle friend.

"Not this time. It's just the three of us, which means we're counting on you."

He looked around. "What do I need to do?"

I wasn't sure, but I had to say something. I decided to tell him that the necklace was magical to make it sound more important. "A magical necklace was stolen, and I'm hoping when you look in the safe that you can either smell or see something with those eagle eyes of yours." Compliments went a long way with him.

He lifted his chest. "Leave it to me."

I smiled. With Iggy tucked away in my bag, the four of us went to the Magic Wand Hotel. The wind had subsided, but the air smelled of rain.

Steve spoke with the desk clerk, who then called Mrs. Coronado to let her know we'd arrived.

Steve faced us. "We're all set. Let's go."

He pressed the elevator for the top floor. I didn't know why I was surprised that she would be in the penthouse suite since she was an heiress, but I was.

"I've never even been to the top floor before." I would have had no reason to stay at the Magic Wand since my own apartment was across the street.

Jaxson smiled. "Enjoy it while you can."

I lightly punched him, though he certainly didn't deserve it. The sheriff knocked on Mrs. Coronado's door, and she answered immediately. The fact her gaze latched onto me, made me feel both welcome and uncomfortable.

She held out her hand. "I'm Alexandria Coronado, but please call me Alex."

Since the client was always right, I did. "Alex, I'm Glinda Goodall and this is my partner, Jaxson Harrison."

She shook his hand. Iggy poked his head out of my purse. "What about me? I'm the most important person here."

I schooled my features, so I didn't chuckle, but the smile on Alex's face implied she'd heard him. I wanted to make certain she had special powers. I lifted Iggy out of my bag. "Iggy here can smell and see a lot. I thought he could investigate the safe."

She smiled at him. "She's so cute."

It always was a bit frustrating when people thought Iggy was a girl. I'd just called Iggy a *he*. Instead of a snarky comment erupting from my familiar's lips, he lifted a claw in what looked like a handshake. That was a first.

"Nice to meet you," he said.

What? Since when was he the gentleman? Iggy must be smitten by her. That shouldn't surprise me since Alex was a beautiful woman.

She took his fingers between her thumb and forefinger and shook it. "Nice to meet you, too."

I had to know. "May I ask you a delicate question?"

She nodded. "Of course."

"As our sheriff explained, I am a witch, but apparently so are you, or did I misread the signs?" Though I don't know how I could. However, it was possible someone had put a spell on her so that she could communicate with familiars—like Jaxson could.

Her shoulders slightly stiffened. "I am, but it's not something I go around announcing."

"I totally understand. Does your necklace have magical powers?"

Her lips thinned. "Why do you ask?"

I lifted the necklace off my neck. "This was a gift from my grandmother. It contains a lot of magic. If anything happened to it, I'd be frantic."

She flashed me a quick smile. "Like I've been. I see. Nothing gets past you. Yes, the necklace possesses some power."

I waited for her to tell me what that power entailed, but I sensed she didn't want to say. In truth, it didn't matter. The necklace was missing, and she needed help finding it.

"Can I have Iggy check the safe?" I asked.

"Sure, but it's empty."

"That works."

The safe door sat open. "I'm not sure what Iggy can find," she said.

"Maybe he'll surprise us." I placed him inside. Even though his eighteen-inch long tail stuck out, he managed to work his way from the left side of the safe to the right. I was proud of his non-random approach.

When he placed his eye close to the lock, he sniffed, and then crawled out. "Someone tampered with the lock."

I hadn't expected that. "How so?"

Iggy looked over at Steve. "If you use a magnifying glass, you'll see bits of what might be gum since it smells like menthol."

I translated what Iggy said to Steve.

"Someone put gum in the lock to prevent it from closing properly?" Iggy bobbed his head once. Steve stepped over and checked it out. He sniffed. "I can smell the menthol." He turned to Alex. "Thoughts?"

Her lips pressed together. "You've spoken with the staff. Did they seem like the type to do this?"

"There has never been a theft in this hotel before."

She turned around, walked over to the chair in the corner, and dropped down. "I need a moment."

The poor woman was suffering. "Steve, did Alex give you the names of everyone in her group?" I kept my voice low.

"Yes. Her husband, son, assistant, and the company's lawyer. That's it."

I was glad it wasn't a large number of people. "When you interviewed them, did any of them seem off?"

He smiled. "You mean, do I think one of them is guilty?"

"Yes. You're a lawman. You must have a gut instinct."

"Since I know you'll ask around, I'll keep my opinions to myself for now."

Iggy cleared his throat. "Can I get a little help here?"

He could have crawled down from the counter, but he wanted the attention. I obliged and placed him on the floor. He might want to investigate further.

"I have an idea." I motioned for Jaxson to come with me to speak with Alex.

There was a small couch across from her chair. "Have you ever done a locator spell before?" I asked her as we sat down.

Her eyes widened. "I'm not really that kind of witch."

Now I was confused. "What kind of witch are you?"

"One who doesn't know how to do spells."

If I had to explain what kind of witch I was, I'm not sure I could be specific. "Have you tried to do any spells?"

"Not really."

I looked up at Jaxson. "My fiancé is not a warlock, but he can hear Iggy talk because I put a spell on him that has thankfully lasted a while now. He's seen me and others do locator spells. It's easy."

"You mean like the one you used to find Rihanna?" Jaxson asked.

"Yes. I will admit I ended up finding her car instead of her, but we did locate her eventually."

"Don't forget that Hugo found Andorra," Steve said as he moved closer to us.

"Hugo?" Alex asked. "Who's he?"

Telling her that Hugo and Genevieve were shape-shifting gargoyles might freak her out. "He is a friend. I'm thinking he might be able to help, too. Do you have a picture of this necklace?"

"Of course." She pulled out her phone and scrolled through some photos. "I'm wearing the necklace in this picture. Does that count?"

I smiled. "It does."

Chapter Three

ALEX HANDED ME her phone to show me the photo of her necklace. It was a string of light pink pearls. "It's lovely."

"Thanks. It was my mother's and her mother's before her."

As I was showing the photo to Jaxson, Iggy crawled over. "Let me see. You might need me to find it."

I swallowed a laugh. "We might."

Iggy studied the picture. "Got it."

"I've never met someone like Iggy before," Alex said.

Iggy perked up at that. "I'm special."

She smiled. "I can see that. Are there more like you?"

He lifted his chest. "Nope. I'm unique."

He was at that. "I'd like to speak with Hugo. I really think he might be able to help you."

She planted a hand on her upper chest as if she was used to being comforted by the necklace, only hers wasn't there, and I felt her pain.

"That would be wonderful. I appreciate anything you can do, Glinda."

I stood. "We'll be in touch."

Once in the elevator, Steve asked if this involved the locator spell?

"It does, unless Hugo or Genevieve have some other ideas about finding Alex's necklace."

"Then I'll let you do your thing. I need to head back to the office and check in with Misty to see if she and her team learned anything," Steve said.

"Thanks." Once outside, Jaxson and I walked down the street to the Hex and Bones with Iggy in tow. I kept my head down, since it had started to drizzle in a typical summer day kind of way.

"Can a spell pinpoint the location of an item?" Jaxson asked. "A necklace might be harder to find than a person."

"Not pinpoint, just give a general direction, unless the witch performing the spell has a clear vision of its location. Bertha might know more." Andorra and Elizabeth's grandmother owned the occult store, and she was a powerful witch.

Inside, we spotted Elizabeth and Bertha, but not Andorra. Hopefully, she was in the back with Hugo. Iggy would be disappointed if his friend was out and about again today.

My familiar crawled out of my purse and down my leg to the floor. He scurried off. "Let's talk to Bertha," I said.

Elizabeth was helping a customer, and her grandmother was at the cash register.

Bertha looked up and smiled. "Glinda, Jaxson, nice to see you again. Andorra is out running an errand with Genevieve."

I stilled. "Is Hugo with her?"

"No. He's in the back and will be very happy to see Iggy."

"Good." Since Iggy was with us, he could communicate with Hugo and translate for us if need be. The only other two people who could speak with the mute gargoyle were Andorra and Genevieve. "Did you hear about the theft at the hotel?"

"Only briefly. What happened exactly?"

Jaxson tapped me on the shoulder. "I'm going to pick Hugo's brain while you chat with Bertha."

"Good idea." I gave her the details. "What do you think?"

"This woman could be successful using the locator spell, but if Alex hasn't done anything like this before, the chances of it working are slim. That being said, we should give it a try since we have nothing to lose."

I must have been holding my breath, because the air whooshed out in relief that she was willing to give it a go. "Thank you. Do you think we can ask either Genevieve, Hugo, Andorra, or Elizabeth to help?"

"Of course, but I'd ask Hugo first. He might be able to give you some special guidance. He's been known to channel other people's thoughts in the right direction. That being said, Elizabeth can help too."

I didn't know that about Hugo's abilities. "Can you collect what we need while I bring Alex back here. She'll pay for whatever we use."

Bertha smiled. "I'd be happy to."

"Tell Jaxson I'll be right back."

"I will."

I hoofed it back over to the hotel, not happy that I hadn't thought to grab an umbrella on the way out of my apartment. I stepped into the hotel lobby, and instead of asking the clerk to tell the vitamin heiress I was there, I marched toward the elevator and rode it up to the top floor. I then knocked on Alex's door.

A young man, about thirty-years-old. "Yes?" He sounded suspicious of me for some reason.

I held out my hand and introduced myself. "I'm here about Alex's necklace."

"Nice to meet you. I'm Alex's son, Gustavo."

Alex appeared next to him. I quickly did the math in my head. Either she gave birth at the age of twelve or Alex was a phenomenon of nature. But that was a discussion left for another time.

"Glinda. Have you learned something already?"

"I hope so." I explained about the locator spell. "It may be our best bet, but don't worry, we'll be there to help you every step of the way."

She looked at her son who shoved his hands in his pockets. She placed a hand on his shoulder. "This is the woman I told you about. She's the witch."

"Ah, yes, the one with the pink animal."

I wanted to correct him, saying that Iggy was more than an animal. He was my familiar, but for all intents and purposes, he was a nine-pound lizard.

"I won't be long," Alex told her son.

"Good luck."

"If you have an umbrella, take it. It's a little soggy out," I warned.

"I hope it won't last," she said as she grabbed one she'd hooked on the inside doorknob.

I shook my head. "It's supposed to be nice later today in fact." At least that was what Jaxson had said.

"Good to know," Alex said.

I said nothing more until we entered the elevator. Then I had to ask. "You must have been young when you had Gustavo." Or had she adopted an older boy? That was most likely the case. Great. Me and my big mouth.

She smiled. "Thank you. Everyone says that. In truth, it's the vitamins that I take that keeps my skin looking young."

"I need to get some of those vitamins then," I mumbled.

She smiled, clearly having heard me. "Start young. It will keep you youthful for a long time."

Oh, how I wished Rihanna were here with me. She'd be able to tell if Alex was telling the whole truth. Vitamins might be a part of Alex's secret to looking young, and surgery could have played a similar role, but somehow I had the sense something else was going on. But what?

The rain had temporarily stopped as we walked down the street. When we stepped into the Hex and Bones, Alex looked around. "This place is really cool."

I'm glad she liked it. "It is special." I nodded to Bertha. "The lady behind the counter owns this place. She's helping us with the locator spell."

"I'm nervous," Alex said.

I never thought I'd hear those words coming from the self-confident mogul. "Don't be. You're in good hands."

Since I didn't see Jaxson, Iggy, or Hugo, I assumed they were still in the back room, readying for the spell. Elizabeth wasn't in the main showroom either, so perhaps she was setting things up.

We headed to the rear room where Elizabeth was putting herbs in a bowl that was surrounded by four stones, each facing in a different direction.

"Everyone, this is Alexandria Coronado—the woman who's necklace was stolen." I turned to her. "This is Elizabeth Murdoch, the owner's granddaughter. And this gentleman is

Hugo. He's mute. Only Iggy, and his host, Andorra, can communicate with him, but he can hear you." She already knew Jaxson.

"Oh."

I wasn't ready to tell her that Hugo was a magical shifter. In a way, it was better that Genevieve, his gargoyle shifter girlfriend wasn't here. No telling what she'd say.

"Just sit over here, and we'll guide you through the process," Elizabeth said.

Alex sat down and leaned over the bowl. "What's in there?"

"Dragon's blood sage with strands of the sweet grass sage in order to bring harmony and protection to both you and your necklace," Elizabeth said.

For some reason, Alex looked up at me. "You've done this before, you said?"

"Yes, though I've never tried to locate an object with this technique—only a person—but if you concentrate, it should work."

"Good." Alex inhaled. "Now what?"

"Light the sage," Elizabeth said. "When the powder catches fire, it will go out quickly to produce a sweet-smelling smoke. Blow the smoke over the rocks until one or more glows. If one illuminates, that's the direction of the necklace. If two of the rocks glow, the necklace is in between them."

"Will the intensity of the light tell me how far away it is? I mean if this rock lights up, there is a whole country north of here."

Elizabeth smiled. "Excellent question, but no. This is where the connection between you and the necklace comes in.

Place either your hand or hands on the glowing rock or rocks and close your eyes."

"Then what?"

"Focus on the pearls and on what your necklace means to you. At that point, your necklace's location will become known to you."

"That sounds too simple. I know I've not done spells before, but this seems a little hokey to me."

Up to this point, Alex had been a good sport. I would have done the spell for her, but magic didn't work that way. "Just try it."

One second Hugo was off the side, and a moment later, he was behind Alex. He placed a hand on her shoulder and then cloaked himself. She looked behind her and then shrugged when she didn't see anyone. Hugo must have lightened up on his hand pressure since she seemed convinced her imagination was in overdrive.

"I light the sage and that's it?" She sounded a lot calmer. Hugo must be doing something to her mind.

"Yes," I said, forgetting to let Elizabeth respond. Whoops.

Alex followed our instructions. When the sage lit and then extinguished, she blew the smoke over the rocks. I held my breath, unsure of whether this would work or not. I didn't have to wait long, because the rock to the south glowed. This was it.

"Place your hand on the rock and picture your necklace and what it means to you," Elizabeth reminded her, her voice soft and assuring.

Alex did so. For the next thirty seconds, she didn't move. I wasn't sure if that was because she was concentrating or if

Hugo was using his influence.

Her eyes sprung open, and then she smiled. "I know where the necklace is."

I hadn't expected that. "Where?"

"In my hotel room."

I tried not to appear disappointed. I also didn't like to be a downer, so I wouldn't say I was skeptical, but I needed to state the obvious. "Are you sure you aren't remembering where you had it last?"

She swiveled around in her chair. Hugo instantly appeared where he had been before he moved behind Alex. "No. The last time I saw the necklace was when I put it in the safe. I think it's still in my room somewhere."

"Can you be positive you didn't forget to put it in the safe this time?"

"I'm sure. It's a ritual I have every night. Trust me." She sounded adamant.

Iggy wagged his tail. "I can look. Maybe you knocked it off the dresser by mistake, and it rolled under a chair."

I loved his enthusiasm, but necklaces didn't roll. "There are maids who clean daily, Iggy. They would have found it."

"Let him try," Alex said. "I might have been distracted when I put it away—or rather when I thought I had put it away."

"It can't hurt, Glinda," Jaxson said.

"Okay."

"You guys go and check," Elizabeth said. "I'll clean up."

"Thank you."

Alex shook her hand. "Thank you. What you did means so much to me."

I wondered if Hugo would be coming with us. He seemed to possess a sixth sense about these things. "Hugo, do you want to join us?"

He shook his head as he looked at Iggy who answered for him. "He doesn't like going out without Genevieve."

That could be because he drew his energy from her. "Okay. Maybe later."

After Alex paid Bertha for the ingredients, Iggy, Jaxson, Alex, and I returned to the hotel. "You're sure you looked everywhere before?" I asked.

"Yes. I'm positive. I wouldn't bother looking again except that I had this overwhelming assurance enter my body that it was there."

I hoped it wasn't Hugo playing tricks with her mind. Just as we stepped off the elevator, the door to her room opened and out walked her son, Gustavo, with another woman.

I expected Alex to be upset that he was still in her room, but she smiled and rushed toward the lady. "Jodi, I didn't think you could make it."

The young woman hugged Alex. "I finished my work early." She looked over at Alex's son. "And I missed my husband too much."

I squeezed Jaxson's hand, thankful we could work together.

Alex turned around. "Let me introduce you to my daughter-in-law. This is Jodi Coronado."

We shook hands and told her our names. The woman was in her late twenties and well-dressed but wore a bit too much makeup for my liking. Her mother-in-law was far more attractive.

Iggy poked his head out and welcomed her, but he received no response. While that wasn't proof Jodi possessed no magical powers, I'd bet that was the case.

"Did you find the necklace, Mom?" her son asked.

"No, but my gut tells me it's in this room."

Gustavo's eyes widened. "Your gut?"

She lifted her chin. "Yes, now if you'll excuse us, we have work to do. After Jodi's long trip, I bet she's tired."

"I am. Thanks." Jodi and Gustavo stepped into the hallway.

I was a little surprised that Alex didn't ask why her son hadn't left after she did. I guess he had free reign to go where he wanted.

Jaxson, Iggy, and I followed Alex inside. Her husband wasn't there, which I found curious. I would have asked, but he could be anywhere, like in the hotel's business center printing something.

Once she closed the door, I let Iggy roam free. Alex glanced around. "I have already looked in every drawer and under the bed and everything, but I'll check again."

"How can we help?" I asked.

"Let's give Iggy a chance first. The room is a bit small," she said.

For a hotel room, it was large, but she probably didn't want anyone looking through her personal items, and I couldn't blame her.

It wasn't but two minutes later when Iggy backed out from under the bed, dragging a necklace. He spun around. "Told you I could find it."

Alex shrieked. "You found it! I love you, Iggy."

"Good job, buddy," Jaxson said.

Alex lifted up her lost item, placed it around her neck, and sighed. "I can't believe I didn't see it when I looked under the bed."

"It was under something," Iggy announced.

"I'll check." Jaxson dropped down onto his stomach. He peeked under the bed skirt, reached in, and extracted a woman's scarf. After rolling over, he stood. "Is this yours?"

"Yes, but I haven't worn it since I've been here. I have no idea how this found its way under my bed."

That sounded like foul play to me, but I'd let Alex figure it out. Bottom line, her necklace had been missing, and now it had been found.

"Any idea what might have happened?" I couldn't help myself. Loose ends bothered me.

"No. I wore my necklace out to dinner. When Ricardo and I returned, I took if off like I do every night and placed it in the safe."

"Who has the safe code?" Jaxson asked.

"Besides me, my husband and son do, but I don't think pink is their color."

I appreciated she was trying to make light of the situation, but something seemed off to me. "I'm glad you have it back."

"Me, too."

"I think the hotel has a safe that might be more secure, unless you want to change the code on this one," Jaxson said.

She smiled. "I'll definitely be changing the code. I might even consider wearing my necklace to bed. Again, thank you for everything. If you ever need a favor, call on me."

"Thanks. Can I ask what your son and wife were doing in

your room?"

She nodded to the computer on the table. "It has all of our company's information. Gustavo often works in here."

That made sense. "I see. So, what's on your agenda for tomorrow?"

I had no idea why I asked. Our job was done, but I had the sense Alex was lonely and wanted to talk, despite being here with her husband and son.

Chapter Four

ALEX SMILED. "WE came to Witch's Cove for a much needed vacation."

If she lived in Atlanta, I would have thought there would be other places to visit. "I know we have a great beach, but why come to our town?"

"I guess you aren't into scuba diving, or you wouldn't ask."

I tried to recall what Dave Sanders had told me about his boat charter business. He ran the dive shop that was located on the other side of the Wine and Cheese Emporium. "You came to explore the caves?"

She smiled. "Yes. There is also a sunken ship, but I read it was placed there for divers to enjoy."

I never liked being underwater because of the sharks, but I saw no reason to bring that up. "Sounds exciting. Is everyone going?"

"We are. My family loves to dive. We go every year, or at least whenever we get the chance. It's one reason why I was in favor of merging our company with a larger conglomerate. I want more free time."

I didn't know she was merging her company. "I hear ya. Be safe since I heard the tropical storm will be rolling in any day."

Alex nodded. "We have some time before it arrives."

Storms were not always predictable. With Iggy secure in my bag, we left. I didn't say anything until we were out of the hotel. "What are your thoughts?" I asked Jaxson.

"This ain't over yet."

I looked over at him. "What do you mean, this isn't over? Alex has her necklace."

"I know, but I got some strange vibes from her son and his wife."

"Like what?" I asked.

"Alex's son and wife almost looked afraid when they saw us get off the elevator."

"I have to agree that he acted a bit uncomfortable, but maybe it was because he never mentioned his wife was coming down from Atlanta. His mom might not be big on surprises."

"True, but that's assuming *he* knew Jodi was coming down," Jaxson said.

"Sounds like a mystery novel to me. You up for some tea?"

His eyebrows rose. "Do you think Maude has more gossip?"

Maude Daniels owned the Moon Bay Tea shop. "No. I just want a chocolate chip cookie to celebrate."

He smiled. "You got it."

The wind was still prevalent, but it looked like the sun was trying to make an appearance, for which I was grateful. At the shop, we found a seat near the window since I loved to people-watch. Most of the families who came to Witch's Cove this time of year just wanted a few days of relaxation at the beach. If I weren't so fair, I might enjoy the sun, too.

Maude came over. "Hello, you two. I heard you have a case."

"We do, or rather we did."

Whoops. We forgot to tell Steve that Alex found her necklace. I needed to tell him that ASAP.

I explained how Iggy located the necklace under the bed in the hotel.

"Are you thinking the owner dropped it, and inadvertently kicked it under the bed?" Maude asked.

"I wish I knew."

No surprise, Iggy took that moment to stick his head out of my bag, probably looking for some accolades. Since Maude wasn't a witch, she couldn't communicate with Iggy. However, she looked over at him and smiled. "Good for you, boy."

"I bet Iggy would like some lettuce as a reward. I know I would like a chocolate chip cookie and a tea."

"You got it. Jaxson?"

"Coffee. Black."

That was his usual. As soon as Maude took off, I pulled out my phone. "We need to let Steve know that Alex's case is closed."

"But is it?"

Why did he keep harping on that? "You're serious, aren't you?"

"Think about it. If we believe Alex, she put her necklace in the safe. That means someone must have broken into the safe and then hid the necklace under the bed. Remember, the lock appeared to be tampered with. I'd like to know who did that, and why did they hide it instead of stealing it."

I blew out a breath. "I was so excited that Alex found her necklace that I forgot someone might have wanted to scare or torment her for some reason."

"Go ahead and call Steve to let him know. If he wants to close the case, that's his choice."

Who was this man? I was the one who didn't let things rest. "Okay."

I called Steve and explained about the locator spell and then how Iggy found the necklace under the bed.

"Well, that was convenient. Do you think Alex made up the story about the necklace being stolen in the first place?"

I chuckled until I realized he was serious. "Why would she do that?"

"I don't know. I'm going to do a little research on her and her company. She might need the insurance money and assumed no one would find it."

"She is an heiress. I doubt she'd try to pull an insurance scam. And if she did, why not hide the necklace in her car instead of her hotel room where it was bound to be found?" But what do I know.

"You're right. I wasn't thinking."

That was a first. "By the way, Alex said her company was merging with another one. I don't know the names of either one though. You could be right. Her firm might be in financial trouble."

"I'll check it out."

Now I was super curious. "Let me know."

"Will do. And Glinda?"

"Yes?"

"Great job."

Wow. Compliments from Sheriff Steve Rocker were far and few between. "Thank you."

I disconnected and told Jaxson what Steve said.

"We'll let him follow up. Even if we wanted to investigate further, without Alex asking us to or providing us with more information, we wouldn't get far."

"No, but maybe you can check out this new merger she spoke about."

"I can try," he said.

"I would have liked to have met the other two people in their group—the assistant and the lawyer. I wonder why Alex's assistant wasn't hovering nearby looking for the necklace? Or have I watched too many television shows?"

Jaxson smiled. "You do have a wild imagination."

Just then, Maude returned with not only our drinks and snacks, but lettuce for Iggy. "Thanks, Maude."

With the topic of Alex's necklace closed, I sat back to enjoy my cookie and drink. When I was only half way through my cookie, my cell chimed, and I checked the ID. "It's a text from Aunt Fern."

"I wonder what she wants?" Jaxson asked.

She rarely called. I scrolled down. "Iggy, you'll want to see this."

He was sitting on my lap eating his piece of lettuce. "What is it?"

"Aunt Fern said that your petition to ban seagulls from the beach has two hundred signatures!" That was the number required in order to take it before the city council.

I suppose if he'd had room, he would have spun around.

"Yes! Goodbye, you dirty Tippy."

I didn't want to get his hopes up. "Getting the petition to rid the beach of seagulls is only the first step. Next we have to give it to the mayor. Then he has to consult with his people."

"Whatever. Let's go now."

Iggy never had learned patience. Hmm. I wonder who he took after? "We have to pick up the petition from Aunt Fern and then walk it over to the mayor's office. We can do that but only after Jaxson and I have finished eating."

He lowered his head. "Okay."

"You do realize it could be weeks before the council meets to vote on this? Even then, I'm not sure if Tippy and his group will comply."

"Then Tippy and I will have a talk."

I didn't even want to know how he would accomplish that since Iggy claimed Tippy didn't talk. "Okay."

I returned to my snack and looked over at Jaxson. "If you want, you can do a bit of computer work while Iggy and I drop off the petition."

He smiled. "I think I'll do that."

Ready to embrace this new mission, we finished up and paid. Our first stop was the Tiki Hut Grill—or rather my first stop. Jaxson smiled and continued on to our office.

Aunt Fern waved us over when we entered.

"You have the petition?" I asked.

"I have it right here. The response has been quite impressive," she said as she handed me the document.

Iggy poked his head out. "Thank you for helping me."

"My pleasure. I wish you luck, but have you thought about what happens when the seagulls leave for another beach?"

"Yes. I'll get some peace and quiet."

Her eyes widened. "You're not afraid of rats?"

Iggy ducked into my purse. I tapped my bag. "Aunt Fern asked you a question."

He emerged. "I hate rats. Why?"

"Why do seagulls exist?" my aunt asked him.

"To torment me."

"Iggy, be reasonable," I said.

"Glinda's right, Iggy. Seagulls have been here long before you were born. Why do you think they exist? By that I mean, what purpose do they serve?"

"To eat and poop."

My aunt nodded. "You're right. That's what they do, but can you guess why we see so many of them on our beaches?"

Iggy looked away. "No."

"Okay, I'll tell you. Their job is to clean the beaches of garbage that people leave behind. Think of them as nature's garbage collectors. Get rid of them and the next group to take over is the rats."

Iggy glanced between me and Aunt Fern. "You're making that up."

My aunt held up a hand. "I am not. Ask Jaxson to do a bit of research. All animals serve a purpose. Without bugs, what would the smaller birds eat?"

"I don't know."

"Nothing. It's why we need them. Bugs may be pests to us, but they aren't to the birds. Some bees sting, but without them, there would be no flowers and a lot of other things."

He hung his head. "And I would starve."

"You could eat lettuce for the rest of your life, maybe. I think bees are needed for everything, though." I really needed to bone up on my science, and it was a subject I liked.

"Are you saying I shouldn't give the mayor the petition?"

"It's up to you," I said. "Why don't you think about it? You need to decide if you want to chance being pooped on by a seagull or bitten by a rat and maybe get some deadly disease."

Of course, I had no idea if iguanas could be affected by a rat bite, but it would be nice if Iggy decided on his own that he wanted to co-exist with Tippy and his friends.

He looked up at me. "Why do you hate me?"

I laughed. "I love you. I'm just trying to educate you. You should actually be thankful that Tippy is here to keep the rats away."

From the way he slipped back into my purse, he was overwhelmed by this new information. I hugged my aunt. "Thank you for everything."

"You bet. It's been interesting to see how many people actually love the seagulls. A lot of the customers I asked to sign the petition were adamant about saving them. They are rather elegant birds."

"Pff," Iggy huffed from inside my bag. "Elegant, my—"

"Iggy!"

He peeked his head out. "Sorry."

He was not in a good mood. "Just remember that we need to preserve nature's balance."

"Whatever."

Arguing with him now would only make things worse. Together, Iggy and I returned to our office. I should be happy the issue with Tippy might soon be resolved, but the whole affair with Alex's necklace still unsettled me.

When we entered, Jaxson motioned us over to his computer. "You didn't take long."

"I'll tell you about it later." I placed my purse next to the chair and sat down. Iggy crawled out and made his way to the top of the desk instead of hiding under the sofa. "You have something to add?" I asked.

"No. I want to see what Jaxson found out."

Now he was interested in the case—a case that was more or less over? Or was he waiting to ask Jaxson to do more research on the value of seagulls? "Okay."

"I didn't have a lot of time, but I found Alex's vitamin company website, and there was a mention of a merger with a large vitamin producer in California."

"That means she was telling the truth."

"Yes, but her website also has a list of employees."

He must have a theory, or he wouldn't be showing this to me. "What did you learn?"

"They've been working on this merger for six months. Apparently, the details have been a bit contentious."

"Were the details between the two companies an issue or did the trouble come from within Alex's company?" It would make a difference.

"I couldn't tell. Alex would know, but she has no reason to tell us." He leaned back.

"What do you think, Detective Iggy?" Iggy's face was practically pressed against the screen.

"I'm thinking Hugo might have learned something when he was messing with Mrs. Coronado's brain."

I hadn't even thought of that. "That's an intriguing concept. Did he say anything to you?"

Iggy turned toward me. "No. Hugo is a gentleman. He doesn't kiss and tell."

"I see." That didn't really apply here, but I let it drop.

Jaxson seemed to be containing a smile. "Why don't you two ask Hugo, and I'll keep digging on my end?" he suggested.

That was his way of getting rid of us. "Are you planning to follow the money so to speak?"

He smiled. "Something like that."

I know I wouldn't get any argument out of Iggy if I suggested we return to the Hex and Bones. "Let's go see your friend."

"Yes!" He then faced Jaxson. "While you're at it, could you check to see if there are any benefits to seagulls?"

Jaxson looked up at me. "I'll tell you later," I said.

"Oh, yeah, and look up monkey bridges, too," Iggy added.

My iguana had lost his mind. "What is a monkey bridge?"

"Aimee told me about them. Monkeys need to cross roads like I do. Roads are dangerous, but more so for me because I can't run as fast as a monkey."

Unless he watched a monkey on television, I doubt he'd ever seen one. "That's where a bridge comes in?" I asked.

"Yes. It's maybe six-inches wide and is strung above the road."

I didn't want to tell him that rats could use it, unless there was no ladder for them to get up there. Iggy could climb anything, so he wouldn't need one.

"I'll look into it, buddy."

"You are the best," my iguana said.

Wasn't I the one about to take him to visit his friend? Sheesh. I never won. Jaxson was his hero.

Chapter Five

I PROBABLY SHOULD have called before heading over to the Hex and Bones to make sure Hugo would still be there, but I didn't think of it before I left. While our local gargoyle had helped us a short while ago, Genevieve might have returned and suggested she and Hugo go for a stroll. If he was at the store, it would be great, and if Andorra was there, it would be an added bonus since Iggy might not want to tell me something that Hugo said. Their bond was tight. If neither were there, I'd pick Bertha's brain.

I entered and immediately spotted Andorra at the checkout counter. Good. She was back. My friend looked up and smiled. I waved and went over.

"I heard you guys did a locator spell while I was out," she said, excitement lacing her tone.

"We did."

"How did it go?"

I hissed in a breath and then flashed her a smile. "Whoops. I should have called Elizabeth to let her know we found the necklace."

Iggy popped his head out. "You mean, *I* found the necklace."

I lifted him out of my bag and placed him on the floor.

"Yes, you did. Is Hugo here?" I asked Andorra.

"He is."

That was all Iggy needed to hear. He took off in the direction of the back room.

"You don't sound all that excited that you and Jaxson just closed a case," she said.

"I'm not sure what I am feeling. I'm happy that Alex has her necklace back."

"But?"

Andorra seemed able to sense things about people. "We never figured out who took it in the first place. Someone put Alex's necklace under her bed, and I want to know who and why?"

Andorra's brows rose. "If Alex is worried about it, I imagine she'll question everyone around her. She might be able to tell who is lying."

"How? Do you think she's like Penny or Rihanna?" I asked.

"Probably not, but you don't succeed at running a corporation unless you're good at reading body language."

"You're right." Andorra's words really soothed me. "You are so right."

"If you need to get back to the office, I can have Hugo return Iggy to your place when they finish their bonding session."

"That sounds wonderful, but I wanted to ask Hugo about Alex, and what he did during the spell. Did he read her mind or control it in some way?" I asked.

"I have no idea, but I'll be happy to ask him for you. If he tells me anything, I'll call you."

That worked since I needed an interpreter anyway. "You are the best, thank you."

Andorra placed a hand on my arm. "The four of us must do dinner soon."

"I love that idea." Too often we'd put it off, and that was wrong. "How about tomorrow night?"

She smiled. "I'll call Drake and see if he can take the time off."

"Great."

Feeling better than I had since I first learned about the theft of the necklace, I headed back to the office. When I arrived, Jaxson was still at his desk.

He looked up. "Did Hugo spill the beans?"

I smiled. "Iggy is still with him, but Andorra will ask Hugo and report back."

"Great. I have to say, you look less stressed."

I told him what Andorra said. "I even suggested the four of us go out to dinner tomorrow."

"Sounds wonderful."

I slid onto the seat next to Jaxson. "Did you learn anything new?"

"I found out that those running Alex's company are competent professionals."

"Good to know. Since you can't get into their financials, we'll never know how desperate she is to merge."

"No." Jaxson turned to face me. "I think we should consider this case closed."

I didn't want to, but we had solved the client's problem. "You're right. Maybe a walk on the beach is in order then. It might give us a hint about whether the storm is near or if it will pass us by."

Jaxson took my hands in his. "It might give me an idea about other things too!"

I laughed then leaned over and kissed him.

"LOOKS LIKE THAT storm my smart brother has been warning us about will soon be here," Drake said as he glanced out the Tiki Hut Grill's glass doors that were facing the ocean.

"Only the outer bands," Jaxson shot back. "Not the main storm."

The tropical storm had veered more toward Texas, which was good for us but bad for them. Aunt Fern had hurricane shutters for the back of the restaurant, but she needed to board up the front if the winds got bad. Hopefully, they wouldn't be needed.

I checked out the view of the beach. The sea was choppy, but it didn't look too treacherous out there. "I guess Dave won't be taking any clients out tomorrow."

"Didn't you say Alex and her family went scuba diving today?" Andorra asked.

"I have no idea which day she planned to go or how many days they were diving," I said. "We've not been in touch since Iggy found her necklace—with the help of Elizabeth and Hugo, of course."

Andorra had not been able to extract much information out of Hugo about his experience during the locator spell, other than he just calmed Alex down. Somehow, I wasn't buying it.

We were mostly through our meal when Aunt Fern rushed over to our table, looking like she'd seen a ghost—okay that was a bad example since she loved seeing ghosts, but she appeared rather distraught.

I sat up straighter. "Aunt Fern, what's wrong?"

She stopped in front of our table, her hands wrung together. "Pearl just called me—from home—and you know what that means."

I had to think. "Something serious happened?"

"Worse. This afternoon, Dave Sanders took your friend, Alex, and her family on a dive expedition."

"Yes, it's why they came here. She wanted to explore the caves and the sunken boat."

Aunt Fern nodded. "Well, when the party returned to the boat, Alex wasn't with them."

I shoved back my chair. "What do you mean?"

"She drowned."

I know I'd just met the woman, but I liked her, despite her slightly cool attitude at first. "How?"

Jaxson placed a hand on my arm. "Thanks for letting us know, Fern."

She nodded and returned to the cashier's counter where people were lined up to pay. I turned back to the group. All three looked upset. "Alex was a good diver. They often went on these excursions. How could she have drowned?"

"I'm sorry, pink lady," Jaxson said.

Even him calling me his pet name didn't help calm me. I shook my head. "She was wearing scuba gear."

"Maybe her air ran out," Andorra said.

"I don't think so," Drake said. "Dave has a timer set on

each tank."

Jaxson's brother and Dave were friends. "Does he keep tabs on everyone's tank levels?" I asked.

"Yes. He knows how long they can be down for," Drake said. "If he needs to, he'll go down to see what is keeping them if they exceed the limit."

Not wanting the rest of the restaurant to hear, I leaned inward. "Aunt Fern didn't say if they found the body."

"Glinda, what are you saying?" Drake asked.

"I don't know. Something isn't right."

"You could ask Steve for the details," Andorra said.

I wanted to, but he would probably be busy interviewing the family members and Dave's crew. "I will, but I don't believe she just drowned."

"The weather turned ugly," Jaxson said. "Who knows what goes on under the surface of the water under these conditions."

Drake shook his head. "Dave would have called everyone in if he thought the Gulf was too dangerous."

I liked how he defended his friend. Since this meal was turning into a small confrontation, I decided to nip it in the bud. "Let's wait until tomorrow to see what the sheriff has figured out." Though I really wanted to rush over to his office right now—assuming he was there. The man had to sleep sometime, though.

That seemed to sober everyone. "Glinda's right," Andorra said. "Let us know what you find out."

"I will."

My friends knew me well. Usually, after we finished our meal, we sat on the outdoor patio to enjoy an after dinner drink, but between the bad weather and what just happened, we decided to call it an early night.

Since I wasn't ready to go to bed, I asked if Jaxson would sit with me for a while.

"Of course."

When we went upstairs, Iggy was on the coffee table instead of at his usual spot by the window. "There's a storm coming," he announced with the authority of a weatherman.

"I know. Are you worried about Tippy and his friends?"

"Worried about them? No, but what if they have nothing to eat?"

That was the definition of being worried. "They are scavengers. They'll find something. There are always the plants next to the office if they get desperate."

"You are a mean woman." He dared to bob his head at me.

"Iggy, don't. I'm not in the mood." I dropped down onto the sofa and Jaxson joined me.

Iggy looked up at me. "I sense something is wrong. You and Jaxson didn't break up did you?"

That was a ridiculous thought. "No! Never. Have you seen us fight before?"

"No, but Hugo says that all couples have a disagreement now and then."

Hugo? He wasn't even human. "I didn't think he left the store, except when he was with Genevieve. Oh, no, did those two fight?"

"They kind of did, but he said he'll patch things up."

"Okay. Good." I couldn't imagine fighting with someone only using mental telepathy.

I looked over at Jaxson and nodded. Iggy would take the news of Alex's death better if my fiancé told him.

"Iggy, we need to tell you something," Jaxson said.

"What?"

"Alex drowned earlier today."

He spun around and faced us. "No, she wouldn't do that."

Clearly, he didn't understand the concept of drowning. "Why do you say that? Did Hugo tell you something?"

"Just that she was troubled."

"Her necklace was missing. Her *magic* necklace. Anyone would be upset."

He dropped down onto the table. "I think it was more than that."

I looked over at Jaxson. "Maybe we should have a word with Hugo."

Jaxson placed a hand on my arm. "Not tonight."

"Why not? Hugo doesn't sleep."

The slightest of smiles crossed Jaxson's lips. "Can you teleport through the walls to ask him?"

"You know I can't. And the store is locked. Which was why you said that. Fine, I'll wait until tomorrow to contact Steve to find out what happened. If he can't help, Hugo and I might have to have a chat."

"I'll help," Iggy offered.

"I was hoping you'd offer since I can't communicate with him."

"I know." Happy he could be useful, Iggy returned to his stool. When he plopped down, he looked like he was ready to sleep. That, or he probably thought Jaxson and I would kiss, which was something he didn't want to see.

Alex's death disturbed me greatly. I was aware that her death probably had nothing to do with magic, but I was hoping Steve would ask for our help any way.

"Do you think Steve will contact us about the accident?" I asked. "Or is he assuming the gossip queens will tell us?"

"If Steve doesn't call, I have a feeling my brother will contact Dave to find out the details. No doubt, his friend will be very distraught. Not only did a person die, his business will suffer from the loss."

"I can't imagine what he's going through. If I owned a charter service, and one of my customers drowned, I'd be frantic to find answers. From the way Drake speaks so highly of Dave, I bet he looked for Alex when she didn't surface."

"I'm sure he did. I heard those caves can be dangerous," Jaxson said.

"I know, but Alex didn't seem afraid of them at all. I'm assuming she was a certified diver."

Jaxson stroked my arm. "Certified or not, currents and caves can get even the best of divers. A jagged rock could have torn her air hose. If she wasn't swimming with anyone, she might not have been able to get back to the surface in time."

I didn't want to think about that. "It's horrific."

"I agree. What you need right now is a good night's sleep."

I looked up at him. "That isn't going to happen."

"What do you suggest?"

"How about if we watch a movie? Maybe I'll fall asleep, and you can spend the night."

He smiled and kissed the top of my head. "I'd like that."

I swear Iggy grunted. Poor thing. Once Jaxson and I married, Iggy might have to get his own room.

Because I thought I'd need some help falling asleep, I retrieved a bottle of my birthday wine and poured us two glasses. I tapped my glass to Jaxson's. "Let's hope…darn. I don't even know what I hope for. If Alex never resurfaced, what can we hope for?"

Jaxson slipped my glass from my fingers and set my drink on the coffee table. "Come here."

Without saying a word, he held me, and I pushed away as much of the anxiety as I could. I never wanted to move, but I knew I had to help bring closure to Alex's family if it was the last thing I did.

Chapter Six

MY BEDROOM DOOR creaked open, and I slightly roused. "Glinda?" It was Jaxson. For a moment, I'd forgotten that I'd asked him to stay over.

I cracked open my eyes. "Yes?"

"Steve is here. He wants to talk to you about Alex's death."

I hadn't even realized it was morning. "Sure. Give me a sec to dress."

Jaxson closed the door. As fast as I could, I tossed on some clothes, not caring if I matched or not. After quickly brushing my teeth and washing my face, I went out to learn about this terrible tragedy.

Steve was sitting on the sofa with a cup of coffee. Never in all the times he'd visited me had he ever accepted a cup of coffee from me. Yet, here he was with one in his hand. Go, Jaxson.

"Steve." I sat on the sofa across from him. Jaxson stepped into the kitchen and returned with a steaming cup for me. I looked up at him and half smiled. "Thank you."

"I'll be brief," Steve said. "Mrs. Coronado, her husband, son, her assistant, and the company's lawyer chartered one of Dave Sander's boats to go scuba diving."

"She told me that was why she came to Witch's Cove."

He nodded. "Did you get the sense she was nervous about anything?"

"No, on the contrary. She said one of the reasons she was merging her vitamin company with some big company was so that she and her family would have more time to do this kind of thing."

"Interesting. When you called and told me that Iggy had found the necklace, did Mrs. Coronado indicate how the necklace ended up under her bed?"

I looked over at Jaxson and nodded. He could always tell when I needed him to continue.

Jaxson moved over to the sofa and sat down. "I think Alex was so relieved to have found her magic necklace that she didn't question how it got there."

I remember something she'd said. "It was under the bed, hidden under a scarf, but Alex told us that she hadn't worn the scarf yet."

Steve pulled out a small note pad. "This implies someone stole her necklace and hid it. Any idea why?"

"That's the question that's been rattling around in my head. I thought it was to upset her." I sipped my slightly cooler coffee, and the delicious bean flavor hit the spot.

"Upsetting her is a far cry from murdering her."

I sat up straighter. "Murder? I thought she drowned."

For the first time in a long time, he looked guilty. "I see the gossip tree didn't hear everything. When everyone in the party but Mrs. Coronado surfaced, Dave became concerned. On each tank is an alarm that lets the person know their air would be running out soon. Since Alex hadn't surfaced, he activated it, but he didn't receive any response from Alex. Highly concerned, he put his assistant in charge of helping the others take off their gear while he went down to the caves to look for her."

"I'm assuming he knows those caves backward and forward," Jaxson said.

"That's what he claims." Steve gulped down the rest of his coffee. "Dave looked everywhere. And that's when he saw it."

"Saw what?"

"Her dive gear."

I must have missed something. "Her dive gear? But not her?"

"Just the gear. The hose was cut."

"Could a jagged rock have caused the hole in the hose?" Jaxson asked.

"No. Dave brought up the gear. The hose had clearly been cut—with a knife."

How horrible. "Did he go back down to look for her?"

Steve nodded. "He did, and he called in the Coast Guard to help. They searched for hours, but they had to call it quits when the currents became too strong. They decided that the impending storm made it dangerous to continue. Considering the weather conditions, the Coast Guard was unable to determine how far away her body had floated."

I became sick to my stomach. "Maybe we can do another locator spell for her." It was probably a dumb idea, but not knowing what happened to her would haunt her poor family.

"Glinda," Jaxson said. "She's gone."

"That may be, but her family deserves closure and a funeral. People need time to grieve." Yes, my parents owned a funeral home, so I couldn't help but spew those sentiments.

"Glinda," Steve said. "Didn't you say that you need someone close to the deceased to do the spell, and that person needed to be a witch?"

"Or a warlock, yes, but if we had her necklace it might help."

"What about her son?" Jaxson asked.

"That's a possibility. If nothing else, performing a spell will make the family feel somewhat useful."

Steve focused on my face for a moment. "You're right. If they are busy with that witchy stuff, they won't be hounding me every few seconds."

Really? "That's not the purpose of doing the spell. We need to find the body."

He held up a hand. "I'm sorry. That was insensitive of me. The family needs to feel as if they are helping. Do you want to ask them now?"

I had nothing else to do. "The sooner the better."

Iggy said he had to come if we were going to do a locator spell, since Hugo might need to be involved, and I agreed. Together, the four of us walked over to the Magic Wand hotel.

After Steve asked the desk to call up to Mr. Coronado's room, we were told to go on up. I honestly had no idea what to expect. The only time I'd seen Alex's husband, he hadn't seemed all that interested in what his wife was going through with regards to her stolen necklace.

Steve knocked, and the husband answered. I had to blink a few times. This guy looked a few years older than when I'd seen him at the front desk a few days ago. I guess losing a loved one could age a person.

Jaxson and I introduced ourselves, and then Steve asked if we could come in.

"Of course. Is there any news on Alex?" His voice cracked.

"No, I'm afraid not, but Glinda, who helped Alex find her necklace, has an idea."

"Anything."

I was pleased he seemed willing to cooperate. "We'll need your wife's necklace to do a locator spell. I have to have something that belongs to her in order to do it."

He shook his head. "I'd like to help you, but Alex locked it in the safe and changed the code."

Guests must forget their code all the time and have to ask the hotel for help. I turned to Steve. "Do you think the front desk has a master code that will open the safe?"

"They might. I'll ask. Be right back."

The Magic Wand Hotel was old, and the owners hadn't embraced technology in every way. I could only hope they had some protocol for something like this.

"Even if we are able to get the necklace, it is necessary for a family member to help with the spell. And that family member needs to be someone who possesses magic—like Alex did." I held my breath hoping his wife had told him that she'd mentioned her witch abilities to us.

"I'm not a warlock."

O-kay. "What about your son?"

He glanced to the side. "He is one, but he doesn't like to admit it. Gustavo begrudges his mother for not embracing her talents and teaching him. He believes he could have been more powerful if she had."

"That is a shame. Do you think he would be willing to help us, though, assuming we can get a hold of the necklace?"

"I'll have to ask him."

Steve returned before Mr. Coronado left. "I'm afraid they can't open the safe unless they hire someone to drill out the lock, and that will destroy the safe, which is something they really don't want to do."

"The safe is useless to them as is, but before we insist they drill open the lock, I might have another way."

Jaxson placed a hand on my back. "Levy?"

He remembered. "Yes. Mr. Coronado, if you could speak with your son, I'll contact someone who might be able to help us."

"Of course, but he's with Dave Sanders, the man who we chartered the boat from."

"Are they looking for Alex?" Steve asked. "I was told that Dave and the Coast Guard had given up the search."

"The weather was better this morning. Gustavo knows where he last saw Alex, and he wants to go down in the hopes of finding a clue as to what happened."

I could figure out what happened. Someone cut her air hose. Needing to get to the surface, she ditched the gear. Obviously, she ran out of oxygen before that and drowned. "I understand. How about we return in an hour or so and hopefully, Gustavo will be back by then?"

"Perfect. I'll give him a call and ask him to return as soon as possible."

I doubt he carried his phone underwater, but hopefully he was on his way back. I probably should have asked Iggy if he wanted to stay and eavesdrop, but if his ability to remain cloaked failed, no telling what might happen—especially since someone on the boat had been the person to cut Alex's hose.

"I'm going to check to see if Dave has returned," Steve said as soon as we left the hotel. "I have a few more questions I need to ask him."

"Okay. I'm hoping Levy knows of someone who can open the safe using his mind."

He hesitated for a second, as if he was searching his memory. "Like that funky heist where the guys could open locks mentally?"

"Exactly. While those particular men are in jail, I'm hoping Levy can find some good warlock who can do the same thing."

He flashed me a smile. "Sounds great. Let me know."

Once outside, Steve went one way, and we went another. "I'll call Levy, and then we need to see if Hugo can help, too."

Iggy poked his head out. "I can translate."

I don't know why he needed to state that again. We always asked him to interpret what Hugo was thinking whenever Andorra wasn't available. "I was hoping you'd volunteer."

On our walk down the street, I called Levy Poole, the powerful warlock who was Gertrude Poole's esteemed grandson. He ran the local coven a few towns over and seemed to know everything about the occult.

"Glinda?"

He didn't have to sound so surprised to hear from me. I'd called him often enough. "Yes. It's been a long time."

"Got a good mystery for me?"

I chuckled. "You have no idea."

Instead of going inside the Hex and Bones, I stopped outside while I continued the call. Jaxson motioned that he'd take Iggy inside since my familiar would want to speak with Hugo.

I lifted Iggy out, handed him to Jaxson and watched as he stepped into the shop.

"Tell me," Levy said.

"This may take a while." I explained about Alex's missing necklace. "She is a witch who helped us locate it. Actually, Iggy found it."

"That sounds like a win."

"Yes, but yesterday, she and her group went scuba diving in the caves, and someone cut her air tube. She's missing and presumed dead."

That resulted in a series of questions. "Tell me what I can do."

I explained my need to retrieve her necklace out of her safe in order to do a locator spell to find her or her body. "We have her husband's permission. Do you know of anyone who can open locks with his mind? And I'm talking about good warlocks, not the criminal kind."

"I might have someone. Give me a bit of time to make some calls, and I'll get back to you."

"You are the best."

Levy chuckled and then disconnected.

I went inside to the Hex and Bones, pleased that we might find someone to help. Bertha was there, but not Elizabeth or Andorra, though they could be in the back room. Since Jaxson was nowhere to be seen, that was where I headed.

When I walked in, everyone was seated facing Hugo. That

was a surprise since I'd not seen that before. Instead of saying anything, I slipped next to Jaxson.

Andorra looked over at me. "Any news on Alex?"

I told her about the cut hose, and the failed attempt to locate her. "Does Hugo know anything?"

Andorra looked up at Hugo and then back at us. "When Hugo was urging her to do the spell, he sensed a lot of anxiety."

"I'm not surprised. She'd never done a spell before, and finding her necklace was very important to her."

Hugo shook his head. Both Iggy and Andorra seemed to listen intently. "Go ahead, Iggy," Andorra said. That was sweet that she was letting him shine.

"She was afraid that someone was out to get her."

"That could mean a lot of things."

Jaxson placed a hand on my knee to indicate he had a question. "Hugo, are you saying that Alex suspected someone wanted to kill her?" he asked.

"Maybe," Iggy replied.

"Who?" I couldn't help but ask.

"Hugo doesn't know."

From the way he was leaning slightly forward, Hugo was telling the truth. I had the sense he wanted to help in any way he could.

"Thank you. We might have a chance to find her," I said. "I know she is most likely dead, but her family needs to find her body."

"What did Levy say?" Jaxson asked.

"He'll call back when he finds someone to open the safe." As if Levy had channeled my mind, my cell rang. "It's him."

Chapter Seven

"GLINDA, I MAY have found someone who can open the safe, but he has one request," Levy said.

"Anything." My leg bounced up and down in excitement.

"He doesn't want anyone to know his identity."

I could understand that. "Okay. How will that work?"

"He'll go to the hotel room, but only you can be in the room. He'll enter, open the safe, and leave. He doesn't want anyone in the hallway watching him."

Since his ability to open a safe with no tools might cause some unscrupulous person to threaten him in order to use his talent, I could understand his caution. "I don't think that will be a problem. When can he come?"

"As soon as you have everything arranged."

I inhaled. "I'll call you when things are set. And thank you. I'd say I owe you one, but by now, the list is already too long."

He chuckled. "Happy to help."

I hung up and told everyone that I needed to go to the hotel alone due to the safe cracker's desire for anonymity. "I'll let Steve know so he can instruct Mr. Coronado and the rest of the group not to interfere."

Jaxson stood and hugged me. "Do you want Iggy to

come?"

I looked over at my iguana. "Do you want to?" I asked him. "You can't say anything or show yourself."

"I can be quiet and invisible."

I wasn't sure why he'd want to do that, but he might prove useful. "Okay, hop in."

As soon as we stepped outside, I couldn't believe how quickly the weather had changed once more. Fickle summer. The once slightly sunny sky looked as if someone had poured gray ink into every cloud. A gust of wind picked up my hair and slapped it across my face. Sheesh.

I ducked my head and barreled toward the sheriff's office. I stepped inside, and near silence surrounded me. "It is bad out there," I complained.

"I heard we're supposed to get up to seventy mile an hour winds," Pearl said.

"In that case, I won't be going for any long walks on the beach until it passes." Full disclosure: I rarely go for long walks unless it is with Jaxson, and only then it's not more than twenty minutes.

Iggy poked out his head. "What will happen to Tippy?"

I thought we'd been over this. "You are really worried about the seagulls? I thought you were the one who was trying to ban them from this town."

"I am, but that was before I learned that rats would take over if the seagulls disappeared."

I guess Tippy was the better of the two evils.

Pearl couldn't hear Iggy's side of the conversation, but she probably could put the pieces together. Trying not to laugh, she pressed her lips together as she held out a plate of cookies.

"These might help."

"Thank you. You are so sweet. I need Steve's help with something. Is he here?"

"He sure is. Go on back."

I found the sheriff at his desk talking on the phone. "I understand," he said as he motioned I take a seat. "I agree, we can't take any more chances. Thank you." Steve disconnected and looked up at me. I swear he'd just aged.

"What is it?" I asked.

"That was the Coast Guard telling us what Dave reported. They can't search any more since the waters are too choppy due to the impending storm."

"I understand. Was Dave able to go down this morning?"

"He was. But Gustavo and he only stayed a short while. They didn't find anything since the visibility was so poor."

"That stinks."

"Any news of finding someone to open the safe?" he asked.

"Yes. That's why I'm here. I'm not sure what good it will do since Alex could be miles away from our coast by now." I normally wasn't the type to give up, but I wasn't feeling optimistic right about now.

"You won't be happy unless you try, you know."

Steve knew me well. "You're right. Levy will send someone over to open the safe under certain conditions." I explained what he told me.

"I can see why he'd want to remain anonymous. What do you need me to do?"

"Keep everyone away from the penthouse floor until I come down to the lobby and give the all clear."

He pushed back his chair. "Can do. Let's go."

On the way to the hotel, I called Levy and told him we'd be ready by the time the safe cracker arrived.

"Good. He'll be there shortly. What's the room number?"

I told him, but I had to shout since the winds had picked up. Worse, it had started to rain again. I was used to sunshine and warm ocean breezes, not hurricanes and stinging rain.

I practically ran to the hotel to keep from getting drenched, though it didn't do much good since I was dripping wet by the time I stepped into the lobby.

Steve turned to me. "Have a seat while I contact the family and ask them to come down here."

I was happy to sit. I opened my purse to check that Iggy was okay. "You dry in there?"

"Yes, but I like water."

He did at that. I often forgot that he was a lizard. Less than five minutes later, Steve returned and motioned for Mr. Coronado, who looked like he hadn't slept since the murder, to sit near me. "Mr. Coronado and his son will remain down here until the necklace is safely in your hands."

"Great. Where is Alex's son?"

"Gustavo and his wife are in the room waiting to let you in. They will then come down to the lobby."

"What about Alex's assistant and the company lawyer?"

"They have been told to remain in their room, which is on the first floor. I'll make sure they don't try to sneak a peek at the penthouse suite."

"Thank you." I took the elevator to the top floor and then knocked on the door. Gustavo, who appeared fidgety, answered. Jodi was standing slightly behind him.

I stepped inside the room. "Before you go, let me ask if you are good with helping out with the locator spell?"

"I can try, but my mom is dead. Does it matter where she is?"

I thought that his reaction was a bit calloused, but that could be my upbringing. "I'm sure it matters to your dad."

"Glinda is right, Gustavo. Besides, Alex deserves a funeral."

Gustavo dipped his head. "She does. Sorry. I'm not myself. I'll give it a try."

"I totally get it. I'd be a total mess if anything happened to either of my parents."

Once they left, I let Iggy out of my bag. "You need to stay hidden, okay?"

"I know what I'm doing."

I'm not sure having him here had been smart, but he often could sense things that I couldn't. Iggy crawled under the bed, which was a safe spot. Not knowing how long this man would take, I borrowed a hand towel to dry off and then sat on the chair to wait.

Even though I was expecting the warlock's knock, the sharp rap took me by surprise. I jumped up and pulled open the door. The person who stood on the other side was rather ordinary looking—thin, slightly balding, and he wore thick glasses. He wasn't at all what I thought he'd look like, though I had no basis for why he should be anything different. "Come in."

He scanned the room, his gaze stopping when he found the safe. "Would you mind sitting on the bed with your back to me?"

I thought he was going a bit overboard since I'd already seen his face, but I wasn't about to complain. "Sure."

I took my seat and waited. I don't know if I thought I'd hear him press the keypad or what, but when he said nothing for a few minutes, I couldn't help but grow impatient. "How long does this usually take?"

He didn't answer. Whatever.

"Ah, Glinda?" Iggy said.

"Yes."

"He's gone."

"What?" I whipped around, and sure enough, the man was no longer in the room.

I went over to the safe to see if he'd been able to open the door. He'd left it open with the pearl necklace sitting inside. I turned to Iggy. "Did you hear him open the room door?"

"No. I was being good and hiding."

"I bet he teleported, which means he could have teleported into the room. I wonder why he knocked?" I pushed away that random thought. It didn't matter who he was or what he could do. All that mattered was that the safe was open with the necklace inside.

I slipped the pink pearls into my purse and then grabbed Iggy. "Let's go do this locator spell."

Once I reached the lobby, Steve strode up to me. "He never showed. I'm sorry."

"Yes, he did."

"Then he must have arrived before we did, because no one entered the lobby after us."

"He might be like Hugo and Genevieve." I didn't want to say too much out loud, not with the family close by.

"Ah, I see. Does that mean you have the necklace?"

I grinned. "I do. Wish us luck that we can find Alex with it."

"I have a feeling you won't need luck," Steve said.

I wasn't quite sure what that meant, but I said nothing. I approached Alex's son. "Are you ready to do this?"

He stood. "I've never done anything like this before, so I can't promise anything."

"Don't worry about that." I figured Hugo would do his magic.

Gustavo spoke a moment with his wife and father and then left with us. The weather had let up a bit, but it was still raining. Thankfully, we only had to walk a half a block. With my head down, and my arms tight around my bag, I strode down the street to the shop with Gustavo right behind me. Even if the rocks glowed, unless Gustavo could focus hard on his mom, I'm not sure what he could say other than she's somewhere west of there—which was the direction of the Gulf of Mexico.

I rushed into the Hex and Bones, careful not to slip on the slightly wet floor.

"Interesting place," Gustavo said.

"It's really wonderful. Let's go into the back where we'll have some privacy."

I led him to the room behind the counter. Jaxson, Andorra, Hugo, and Genevieve—who was a surprise guest—were there.

"I haven't seen you in a while," I told her.

"Hugo thought you all could use my expertise."

I didn't know what expertise she was referring to, but I

thought it best not to say anything in front of Gustavo. I introduced him to the gang. "All have magic, except for Jaxson, who only has partial magic."

"Nice to meet you." Gustavo looked around. "What do you need me to do?"

I extracted the necklace from my purse and set down my bag to allow Iggy to crawl out, which he did. Hugo walked over to him, and when he gathered up Iggy, my heart warmed.

Just like when Alex had come in here looking for her necklace, the bowl with the same ingredients as before sat on the table and was surrounded by stones. Andorra motioned Gustavo to take a seat and then explained what he needed to do.

I placed the necklace next to him. "When you are concentrating on your mom, hold this. I know it was dear to her," I said.

"Okay."

The door opened, and I was a bit surprised when Steve and Nash both walked in. I hoped their presence didn't add to Gustavo's stress.

"I light the stuff in the bowl?" He looked up at Andorra.

"Yes."

Gustavo had a good memory since he went through the steps without asking any further questions. When he held the necklace in his hand and closed his eyes, Hugo—and Iggy—disappeared. I had to assume that Hugo was standing behind Alex's son. Whether he was helping him focus or trying to read his mind, I don't know.

I returned my gaze to the stones, but none lit up. Wasn't he concentrating? His mother was somewhere.

Wait. One stone to the south flickered and then went out. I looked over at Andorra, hoping she would understand what that meant.

About a minute later, Gustavo opened his eyes and leaned back. "I'm sorry. It's not working."

My natural instinct was to ask him to try again, but if I had been trying to connect with my mother's body, I might not have been able to concentrate either.

"I understand. Thank you for trying."

Gustavo shoved back his chair a second after Hugo reappeared with Iggy in his hands.

"Excuse me," he said. Clutching the pink necklace, he rushed out of the room.

I waited for someone to say something.

"That was a bust, right?" Steve asked.

Darn. I wanted Steve and Nash to witness a successful locator spell, but this had not been a success. "I'm afraid so."

"Now what?" he asked.

"I wish I knew." I looked over at Hugo. Maybe he'd connected with Gustavo.

"Hugo knows," Iggy said, acting as if his good friend was some all-knowing being. Come to think of it, he might be.

"Tell me."

"The necklace was a fake," Iggy announced.

"That's ridiculous. It was the one in the safe."

Andorra stepped over to Hugo and communicated silently with him. She eventually turned around. "Just as Iggy said—or rather as Hugo said—the necklace is a copy of the original."

My mouth dropped open. "Holy moly. That makes sense. It's why we found it under the bed. Clearly, someone planted it there." Then reason intruded. "But if that were the case, how could Alex have psychically connected with a fake?"

Andorra looked between Hugo and Genevieve. Genevieve placed a hand on Hugo's arm. Perhaps they could communicate faster that way.

"We think that if the desire is strong enough, even a replica can act like the sought after item—energy wise," Genevieve said.

That didn't make much sense, but I wasn't as knowledgeable about the occult as those two were. "You're saying it is a replica, but that Alex connected with it because of her being a witch?"

"Not exactly, but close enough."

"Where's the real necklace?" Nash said.

Good question. "Find that, and we might find the killer." Or at least I hoped.

Chapter Eight

EVERYONE GRABBED A chair and formed a circle in order to brainstorm our next step. A murder had occurred right off the coast of our town. I wasn't sure if our sheriff's department was responsible for finding the murderer or if the Coast Guard would say it was their jurisdiction, but since Alex and her family were diving within a mile of the shore, they weren't in international waters. If I had to guess, I'd say this would be Steve's case.

"Do we think the location of the real necklace will lead us to the murderer?" Steve asked.

"How about I find out?" Genevieve asked.

"How are you going—"

I wasn't able to finish my sentence, because Genevieve disappeared on us. What else was new? I looked over at Steve. He never liked it when she did that.

"We need to train her not to run off like that," he said.

I smiled. "Good luck with that."

"She's impulsive," Iggy said, clearly telling us what Hugo had relayed.

"Hugo, do you know why she left or where she is going?" I could guess, but I wanted his opinion.

He looked over at Andorra, who answered. "She wants to

find the real necklace."

"I figured. I suppose if anyone can find it, it would be her or Hugo. Here's the problem as I see it." I turned to Steve. "Suppose Genevieve comes back and says that the assistant stole the necklace and replaced it with a fake. What then?"

"As long as Genevieve doesn't take it, it might help us figure out who cut Alex's hose," Steve said.

"Being in possession of the necklace won't prove anything other than he or she is a thief," Nash added. "The murder and the theft are probably independent of each other."

"I agree with Nash," Jaxson said. "Let's pretend that the lawyer wanted to give a present to his new woman, and he thought the necklace might be just the thing. He steals it, replaces it with a fake, and then Alex is killed by someone else. No connection."

Steve nodded. "In retrospect, we should have asked Gustavo what kind of magic that necklace possessed."

"If he is connected with the theft, he'll claim he has no idea," I said. "Or else he really doesn't know. When I asked Alex, she was tight-lipped about it."

Nash pushed back his chair and Steve followed suit. "I think it's time we find out," Nash said. "I'm not claiming it will help us solve Alex's disappearance, but it might."

I wondered why he also said Alex had disappeared instead of saying she was murdered? I will admit disappearing sounded nicer.

"If you see Genevieve," Andorra said. "Please ask her to return."

"We will," Steve said. "I suggest you all go home and hunker down. No telling when it will be too dangerous to even cross the street. Downed power lines can kill."

Wasn't he the cheery one? I guess that meant at least part of the tropical storm was headed our way. Darn. "Thanks."

I didn't want to leave just yet. We had too much to discuss, but I could hear the winds outside, and they were rattling the store windows. No doubt we were in for a good thrashing.

As soon as our law enforcement left, I turned to Hugo. "Can you sense where Genevieve is? You two seem to be psychically connected."

He shook his head, but I didn't believe him. I turned back to Andorra. "If Genevieve tells you anything, text me, okay?"

"I will, but we're going to close soon. I don't want my grandmother here when it turns ugly."

"I understand." While I didn't relish getting wet, we didn't have a choice since I'd forgotten my umbrella. "Jaxson, do you have any suggestions where we should stay tonight? Aunt Fern has a closet full of candles should the power go out. Or is your place better?"

"Your apartment has more perks. For starters, we won't starve to death since there is a full restaurant downstairs. But if we do stay at your apartment, we should ask Rihanna to join us. Being alone in Drake's building would be scary."

"Absolutely."

As quickly as we could, we dashed across the street and hightailed it to the Tiki Hut Grill. Since I didn't want to traipse water through the restaurant, I unlocked the side door that led to the hallway and entered. I swiped a hand down my wet face in order to see.

"Let's get dry and then we can see about those candles

should we need them," I said.

He smiled. "Sounds romantic."

Iggy popped his head out of my bag. "I'm going to stay with Aunt Fern. You guys kiss too much."

I laughed. "Suit yourself."

At the front door to my apartment, I let Iggy escape to a more peaceful environment. I was happy that he and Aimee had patched things up between them. How long that would last, I didn't know. Every time Tippy did something, Iggy couldn't keep from talking about it—at least to us.

Once inside the apartment, I changed into dry clothes. Since Jaxson kept a spare set of clothes at my place for emergencies, he also changed.

"I'll get the candles," he offered since he'd finished before me.

"Okay."

I had the best fiancé. The wind buffeted the windows, but from the snippets of news I'd caught during the day, the majority of the storm would pass us by. That didn't mean we wouldn't lose power. Heck, it could be bright and sunny, and then the power could go out, but during a storm, the probability increased ten-fold.

Jaxson returned with four candles. "Even if we have power, maybe we should light these," he said.

I smiled. "I like it, but Rihanna might feel a little uncomfortable."

"Give her a call."

I dialed my cousin's number. "Hey, Glinda."

"Jaxson is over at my apartment, and we didn't want to leave you alone. Do you want to stay here tonight? I have a sleeping bag you can use."

"I appreciate the offer, but Gavin came home for the weekend, and his mom invited me to stay at her place. Her house is a bit sturdier."

I chuckled. "That sounds great. Stay safe."

I was sure Rihanna decided to stay with Gavin not because of any storm. "She's safe and sound with Elissa and Gavin," I relayed to Jaxson.

"Good. Now how about I make some popcorn, and you pick the movie?"

"Sounds great. I think we need storms more often." I was hoping the winds would keep my mind off of what happened to poor Alex.

I found a movie I thought we'd both like while Jaxson made the popcorn and fixed some drinks. "Do you think Steve will ask for any more of our help in figuring out who killed Alex?"

He placed the bowl on the living room coffee table and returned to the kitchen, probably to get the drinks. "Magic wasn't used to cut the air hose," he called out.

"True, but Alex was a witch, and the mystery of who stole her necklace hasn't even been solved. Speaking of the pilfered pearls, I wonder what Genevieve has been up to?"

"Andorra told us she was going home early. She might not know what Genevieve found out until tomorrow," Jaxson said.

"That's true."

As if we'd conjured her, Genevieve popped up in my living room, and I thought my heart was going to stop. I planted a hand on my chest. "Genevieve, you scared me."

"Sorry. I don't know how to make a better entrance."

"You could try appearing on the other side of the door and knocking." I said that in the nicest of tones, but she winced, which made me think I'd failed.

"Okay."

I cleared my throat. "Do you have news about the necklace—the real one, I mean?"

"No, but it wasn't from lack of trying. I listened in on a few conversations, but no one was talking about it."

That made no sense. "Gustavo didn't even tell his dad that the necklace in the safe was a fake?"

"Not while I was there."

I looked over at Jaxson. "What do you think that means?"

He shrugged. "Is it possible someone outside of the family stole the necklace? If Alex wore it to dinner, some thief could have decided he wanted it. It looked expensive."

"I imagine it would bring a lot of money, but would a thief make a copy?"

Jaxson leaned back in his seat. "Probably not."

"We could make a wanted poster and put it up everywhere in town," Genevieve said.

"We could, but if we don't have a sign, the thief might think it has been found. Then he or she might slip up and say something about it. That's assuming Gustavo keeps his mouth shut about it being a fake."

She nodded. "Okay. I can go back and see if they spill the beans."

I loved how she'd picked up on our idioms so quickly, especially considering she hadn't been in her human form for years. "Wait a minute." Genevieve didn't need to eat or sleep, but cloaking herself could be a hardship on her body. "Does remaining invisible take energy?"

"Yes, it does."

"How about if you wait until we need you? I want to see how the sheriff wants to handle this case first." That didn't make a lot of sense, but I feared she'd appear at the worst moment and ruin a plan the sheriff had concocted.

"Okay."

"Thank y—and she's gone." I turned to Jaxson. "Do you think she'll ever stop disappearing like that?"

He smiled. "Nope."

"That's what I thought."

He grabbed a handful of popcorn and stuffed it in his mouth. The lights flickered, and I stiffened.

"Relax. This building has been through a ton of storms," he assured me.

"I know, but for a moment I thought maybe Nana had come to give me a hint about this case." My grandmother often showed up in her ghost form at the most random times.

Jaxson wrapped an arm around my shoulders. "We'll figure out what happened. Eventually."

"Assuming Steve lets us participate."

"Our ace in the hole might be Dave. He'll be asking questions. If he learns something, he'll probably tell my brother."

I nodded. "And Drake will tell us."

"He will." I wanted to put this whole Alex thing to rest for the night and enjoy a movie and some popcorn with the man I loved, but my brain wouldn't shut off. "Who do you think killed Alex?"

Jaxson swiveled to face me. "You can't let it go for one night?"

"I want to. I do, but I can't."

He knew when he was defeated. "Okay. How about this? We take ten minutes to list the suspects of the necklace theft, and then we list who might have killed Alex. After that, we stop for the night. Okay?"

I could tell that was all he was willing to give. "Deal."

I jumped up and found a notebook that had some unused paper in it. "Okay, let's start with her death. Who was on the boat?"

"Mr. Coronado, Gustavo, the assistant, and the lawyer," he said.

"Not Gustavo's wife?"

"No. So, who do you think would want her dead?" he asked.

Sadly, I had no suspects. "I don't know, and I'm not sure how we can find out."

"This proves we need Steve. Since Alex and her group are not from here, I highly doubt the gossip queens know anything either unless Steve wants them to know."

I shook my head. "He won't say anything if the investigation is underway. I feel sorry for Alex's family. The innocent ones will be stuck here for a while."

He snapped his fingers. "Tomorrow, we can go to Steve and offer Genevieve as our secret weapon if and only if he lets us help."

My heart sang. "You are a genius."

Jaxson grinned. "I am at that."

After I thanked him appropriately, I turned on the television, ready to relax and enjoy a good movie.

Chapter Nine

THE NEXT MORNING, after a fairly restless sleep, I woke up to Jaxson carrying in a breakfast tray. Okay, he might have gone downstairs for the breakfast, but the thought was wonderful.

"This smells divine," I said.

He placed it on my bed. "You were up and down a few times last night, and I thought you could use a good breakfast."

"Thank you, but what about you?"

"I ate already." He nodded to the window. "Storm's gone."

I looked outside. "So it is." I dove into my eggs and then my English Muffin. "Did Iggy come home yet?"

"He did. He's waiting patiently for you to get up."

Iggy was never patient, but maybe he was maturing. "It's not that late."

"Not *too* late."

Jaxson and I chatted until I finished my meal. "Thank you. Let me get ready, and we can see how Rihanna's evening went—assuming she's back from Gavin's."

"I'll take the tray downstairs."

While he did that, I cleaned up and changed. Sure

enough, Iggy was on the coffee table waiting for me. "Did you and Aimee have a good time?"

"Kind of. I didn't like all the wind."

"If I only weighed nine pounds, I wouldn't like it either."

"I hope Tippy was safe."

Who was this animal? One minute he wanted to get rid of Tippy and the next he didn't want him harmed. "I'm sure he is. Are you coming with Jaxson and me to the office, or do you plan on scouring the beach for your feathered friend?"

"He's not my friend. I'm going to the office with you guys."

"That works."

Once Jaxson returned, the three of us took off. What I didn't expect was to find a young woman sitting at the top of the steps. "Do you recognize her?" I whispered to Jaxson.

"Nope. Let's find out what she wants."

We climbed the stairs. As we neared, she stood. "Can we help you?" I asked.

"Are you Glinda and Jaxson?"

"We are."

"I was Alex Coronado's assistant."

I almost shouted for joy, until I realized the pain this woman must be in. "Please come in."

"Can I fix you a coffee?" Jaxson asked once she was seated.

"Yes, please."

Rihanna must not be back yet, or she would have answered the door. I placed my purse on the floor. "Ignore my pink iguana."

Naturally, Iggy took offense. He crawled out and gave me the stink eye. "You could have told her I was special."

At the moment, I wasn't ready to talk to my iguana if our guest wasn't a witch. "I didn't catch your name."

"Oh, I'm sorry. I'm Nina Stamos."

"I'm glad you stopped by. How long have you worked for Alex?"

"Six months."

Chances were, she didn't have anything to do with Alex's death. "Do you know anything about what happened to your boss?"

"No. That's why I'm here. I was hoping you would know something. Gustavo told me that you found the necklace."

"Actually, my iguana found it."

If he could have crossed his arms in an arrogant pose, he would have.

"I heard it was a fake."

News traveled fast. If Gustavo had been involved in any funny business, would he be giving out that detail? "According to a local warlock, it wasn't the original one, but I can't say for sure. No one has found another one have they?"

"No."

"Any idea who might have taken the real pearl necklace?"

"No."

She wasn't very helpful. Jaxson returned with three steaming cups of coffee.

"Cream or sugar?" he asked her.

"Just black, thank you."

"Nina, you were on the dive boat the day Alex drowned—or rather was killed, right?"

"I was." She wasn't the most forthcoming person.

"Did you notice anything strange?"

"No, and I've gone over it my head a hundred times."

"Did Alex have any arguments with anyone while she was here?" Jaxson asked.

"Not really arguments, but the whole trip down to Florida, Mr. Coronado and Gustavo were trying to convince Alex not to merge our company with Alfa's Vitamins."

"Why is that?" Jaxson asked.

"They thought—rightfully—that if Alex agreed to the merger, that the Coronados won't have as much say so in the running of our company."

I didn't get the sense that Alex's husband was the domineering type, but I might have misjudged him—or was it the son who wanted to have more control? "Who really ran the company?"

"Oh, Alex did. She started Herbal Reliance twenty years ago. At the time, Mr. Coronado worked as a marketing manager for another company. When Herbal Reliance started to grow, Alex needed help, so she hired her husband."

Even though I had come up with the idea of The Pink Iguana Sleuths, Jaxson and I came on board at the same time. He often said it is my company since I'm the witch, but I always listened to his suggestions.

"Did he resent being second fiddle to Alex?" Jaxson asked.

Nina looked down at her fingers and picked at one of her nails. "Kind of. He thought that because he was the man that his word should be the final one."

Ouch. "What about Gustavo? When did he start working for the company?"

"I don't know. He worked there before me."

"What are your thoughts on him?" Jaxson asked.

"What do you mean?" Nina sipped her coffee.

"Bottom line, I'd like your take on whether Gustavo would be capable of cutting the hose on his mother's tank?"

"Gustavo? No! At least I don't think so. There's no motive to do so. It's not like he wants to take over the business sooner rather than later. In all honesty, I find him to be a bit lazy."

That was an interesting take. "What did Alex think of him—as far as him being an employee?"

"She was frustrated. Gustavo wasn't the best at following through on her ideas."

If I had to choose between the dad and the son, I'd say the dad had more motive to kill Alex. "And the lawyer who came with you?"

"Dante Diaz. Have you met him?" We both shook our heads. "He's nice, but rather aggressive, which is what Alex wanted. Big business is tough. I don't think Herbal Reliance has been sued, but if they ever are, they'll need a shark for a lawyer."

"Would Dante have any reason to harm Alex?" Jaxson asked.

"No. He told me that when he agreed to work at the company, he had like five other job offers. If the merger had gone through, Dante probably would be let go, because the larger firm has their own lawyers, but he wasn't worried. He could get a job anywhere."

That was interesting. "Would it be fair to say that Alex would basically be selling her company to Alfa's Vitamins?"

"I guess, except that besides Dante, we would all be keeping our jobs. I loved the idea of the merger, because it meant

Alex would have more free time. And more free time for her meant less work for me." Her eyes widened. "Not that I didn't like working all the time, but I wasn't going to complain about time off."

I polished off my cup of coffee. That had really hit the spot. "How would you describe Alex as a boss?"

"Good, though I had heard horror stories about her. No one had lasted more than a couple of months as her assistant."

"Why is that, do you think?" I'd been lucky with my employment since I have liked everyone I've ever worked for.

"She demands perfection. And no, I don't deliver all the time, but I am a very detail-oriented person. My mom is an accountant, and my father is a heart surgeon. Mistakes are not tolerated in my family."

"I can see why Alex keeps you. And I can understand how her son's less than focused attitude would bother."

"That's true, but she wasn't one to complain, though I could see her frustration rise at times. Alex was a private person, so she didn't say much, at least to me."

At the moment, it didn't seem obvious who might have wanted to kill Alex. "This is a crazy, crazy theory, but would Alex have done this herself?"

"What? Alex commit suicide? Never. She loved life. Just look at her. She's amazing."

"True, but hear me out. Maybe she wanted people to think she'd died. Would that have served any purpose?"

"No, the merger couldn't go through without her signature, and it was Alex who wanted it."

That blew that theory. "Any other idea who might have wanted to harm her?"

"Not really. Even if I could come up with a name, they weren't on the boat with us. The captain and his crew all stayed on board. If anyone else went underwater, I never saw them."

"Nina, did your party stay together for the most part?" Jaxson asked.

"No. We all started out at the sunken ship, but then we kind of went our way after a while."

"Are you a certified diver?" I asked.

"Yes. We all are PADI certified. Alex loves to dive. I think that was one reason why I was hired. I'm from Miami and learned to scuba dive there."

"You sound like a perfect fit for her. Now that Alex is gone, what are you going to do?"

She shrugged. "Once Alex is declared legally dead, I imagine there will be a transfer of power to her husband. We haven't always seen eye-to-eye, so he won't be hiring me as his assistant."

And there it was. Motive number one for it being the husband, or was it number two? That didn't mean he was guilty, but at least it made sense for him to kill his wife. He wanted to control the company. "How would you describe their marriage, aside from their business association?"

Nina leaned back in the chair. "That's hard to say. I only saw Alex professionally. I always believed that Mr. Coronado was in love with his wife. He often commented that he thought Alex was the most beautiful woman in the world."

"She is pretty for sure, and a lot younger."

Nina picked up her cup, but when she saw it was empty, she set it down.

"Can I get you another one?" Jaxson nodded to her empty coffee.

"No, I'm good."

"I must not be good at judging age, but Alex looks to be in her forties, which doesn't make sense if Gustavo is her biological son," I said.

"Alex is fifty-four."

I whistled. "I have to buy some of those vitamins."

She smiled. "I take them religiously and so does Mr. Coronado, but they don't seem to work on us as well as they do on Alex."

"She must have had good genes."

"Definitely."

"You didn't see any other divers down there?" Jaxson asked.

Nina drew in her bottom lip. "Actually, I did. There were two people on the other side of the caves, but I don't remember them coming close to us. They certainly didn't check out the shipwreck when we did."

I'd have to ask Dave Sanders what other groups were diving that day, assuming he knew. "What is your theory about what happened to Alex?"

"I have no idea. I'm devastated, and I want to help in any way that I can."

"How can we get a hold of you?" Jaxson asked.

Nina gave him her phone number.

If Nina was Alex's personal assistant, she might know why Alex's necklace was magical. "Nina, do you know what was so special about Alex's necklace?"

"Special? I mean it was her mom's and her grandmother's."

"Did it contain magic?"

Her laugh sounded nervous. "I don't believe in magic."

That put an end to that conversation. "I see. Since you have to stay in town for a while, please keep your ear to the ground, and let us know if anything sounds suspicious."

She stood. "I will and thank you."

As soon as Nina left, I turned to Jaxson. "Thoughts?"

"I think I'll get the white board out so you can list your suspects."

I smiled. It always was easier when I could list my possibilities. Just as Jaxson disappeared to retrieve the board, Rihanna came in. "Hey, I see you weathered the storm," I said.

"Yeah, it wasn't much of a storm, though. Sure, the windows rattled, and the power flickered, but otherwise, we were all safe. You?"

"The same."

Iggy came out from under the sofa. "I'm glad that Nina girl is gone so I can talk."

I chuckled. "She couldn't have heard you anyway."

"I know."

"Who's Nina?" Rihanna asked.

We had so much to catch up on. "Put your stuff down, grab a drink, and come on out. We've learned a lot."

Jaxson came out with my white board, and Rihanna's eyes widened. "I see you are determined to find out who killed Alex."

I'd spoken with Rihanna a few times about the case. "We are."

Chapter Ten

IT TOOK QUITE a while to bring Rihanna up to full speed. During our investigation, either she'd been at school or with Gavin and hadn't joined us. The few short phone calls hadn't been enough to tell her everything.

"I can see I've missed a lot," she said.

"Yes, and I wished you'd been with us. I have a feeling several of the people involved weren't telling the whole truth about what happened that day."

"Have you spoken with Dave?" she asked.

"No, but I bet Drake knows something." I looked over at Jaxson. "Do you think your brother can get away and chat for a moment?"

"I'll go downstairs and ask him. If he has no one to man the store, I'll stay down there."

"As always, you are the best."

He grinned and then headed down the interior stairwell. While I waited for either Drake or Jaxson to come up, I set up my whiteboard, and then listed the possible suspects. Those who had been on the boat were my number one suspects. I then listed Alex and the two unknown people who'd been diving nearby. I believed in being thorough.

Rihanna studied it. "Alex is dead. Why list her?"

"Suicide maybe?"

"She wouldn't have been so frantic about her necklace if she was that depressed."

"Maybe not."

Before we could discuss anything further, Drake came up from downstairs. "Jaxson told me you spoke with Alex's assistant."

"Yes, but she didn't have much to add. Have you spoken with Dave?"

"Only about three times since last night. He is a mess. I keep telling him it's not his fault, but he feels as if he could have done more."

"What could he have done? Even though Alex might have been using his equipment—assuming she didn't bring her own gear—it wasn't his fault someone cut her hose," I said.

"I told him that multiple times, but I think that until he learns what really happened, he'll blame himself."

Poor Dave. His whole business was on the line. Losing a customer would not bode well for him. "Does he have any idea how it happened or who might have had it in for her?" I was hoping there had been an altercation before they dove into the water, even though Nina didn't think there had been.

"Not really. All he said was that her son was not happy that he had to be there. He didn't say why he wasn't up for scuba diving, but Alex insisted that the family be together. A little later, she mentioned something about selling her company, so they'd have more time to spend together, and it was the husband who exchanged some hushed words with her."

"Just so you know, it's more of a merger than a sale, but

yes, she wants the free time."

I motioned for my good friend to take a seat. "Did Dave say if he saw anyone else out there? I imagine the caves are a popular destination."

"He noticed a small boat off in the distance. It wasn't a charter, but he said they were pretty far from the caves to be exploring them."

"Then why go down there?" Rihanna asked.

Drake shrugged. "I've never scuba dived so I can't say what's down there. You'd have to ask Dave."

"Where did Dave find Alex's gear? In the caves or near the sunken boat?"

"Actually, it was on the far side of the caves. Dave said that there is an entrance and an exit to these caves. It's kind of a passageway that goes from one side to another."

If that was the case, was it really a cave? I thought caves were one-way structures. "Thanks. Is Dave at his shop?"

"I couldn't say."

Drake left, and a minute later Jaxson returned. "Learn anything?" he asked.

"Not much, but I think we should touch base with Dave." I went over what his brother said.

"Don't you think Steve will try to find out the identity of the other group who was scuba diving nearby?" Rihanna asked.

"I hope so, assuming he knows about them, but until he asks us to help, we need to let him do his thing."

Jaxson's eyes widened. "Who are you, and where is the real Glinda Goodall?"

"You are so funny."

Before I could suggest we check with Dave, someone knocked on our office door. Usually people just walked in, but apparently, this person didn't know the protocol—or read the sign.

Rihanna beat me to the punch and opened it. "I'm looking for Glinda," the deep voice said.

I stepped forward. "I'm Glinda."

A large, beefy man with short dark hair and dark sunglasses stood in the doorway. To say he was intimidating would be an understatement. Thank goodness, Jaxson was there. My fiancé was quite skilled in the art of fighting—another long story.

"I have information about Alex. May I come in?"

If I said no, he could barge his way in, however, his mention of Alex had me curious. "Sure."

The man stepped into the middle of the room. "My name is Geraldo Ortega. I'm Alex's bodyguard."

Why didn't he say he used to be Alex's bodyguard instead of saying he was currently her bodyguard? I guess he hadn't come to grips with her death yet. "This is my partner, Jaxson, and my cousin Rihanna."

Mr. Ortega nodded instead of shaking hands. "Alex mentioned you."

"I'm sorry for your loss."

"Thank you, but Alex isn't dead."

My heart squeezed so tight, my knees nearly buckled. Jaxson knew me well enough to know that I often needed a little help when I was told something shocking.

He wrapped an arm around my waist. "How about we all take a seat? I certainly would like an explanation."

"Of course, but time is of the essence."

Now he was being mysterious. "Why?" I asked as the four of us moved over to the sofa area. Once I was seated, Jaxson dragged over his office chair. We really needed to redecorate in order to accommodate more people.

"I'll let Alex explain in more detail, but she really needs her necklace back. She told you that it has magical powers, and it's those powers that keep her healthy."

"I had no idea that was what her necklace could do."

Iggy decided to crawl out from under the sofa and prance up to the large man. "The necklace I found was a fake," he announced.

I waited for Mr. Ortega to respond, but he did not. He merely glanced at Iggy, and then stuck his hand in his pocket. "Here is the combination to the safe in Alex's room. If you could retrieve the necklace and give it her, she'd be forever grateful."

Wow. My mind couldn't quite connect the dots. "Let's start with how is Alex alive, and then I'll tell you about the necklace."

"Can you get the necklace first. Please. Then I'll tell you about Alex, I promise."

He sounded pretty desperate. "I'm sorry, but the necklace Alex put in the safe was a fake."

"That's not possible."

"But it is." It also seemed rather impossible that Alex was still alive. I explained our theory as to why Alex was able to do a locator spell on a fake necklace.

"I see," Mr. Ortega said. "How again are you so certain it isn't real?"

I wanted to say that Hugo, who was a talented gargoyle shifter, sensed it. Instead, I told him that Gustavo was unable to do the locator spell for his mom because the necklace wasn't authentic. "The person who deemed it fake is reliable."

His lips pursed together. "Regardless, I'd like the fake one to give back to Alex. I'll let her decide if it is or isn't real."

I couldn't blame him for not believing me. "Okay, but why don't you go to her room and get it yourself? You are her bodyguard, and you have the combination."

"Alex wants everyone to believe she is dead. If I have the code, they'll ask me how I have it."

This could be tricky. "How will I explain that I have the code?"

"Tell them that Alex gave it to you before she went scuba diving."

I shook my head and explained that was impossible. I didn't reveal that the man Levy sent had been able to open the safe with his mind. "Mr. Coronado and Gustavo know we had to bring in a specialist to open the safe in the first place. If Alex had given me the code, I would have used it then."

"I see the problem," he said. Mr. Ortega tapped the arm of the chair. "I guess I could sneak in, assuming I can get into the room."

I looked over at Jaxson. "I think the sheriff can help you, but we'll have to tell him the truth."

"Can you trust him?" he asked.

"Completely."

Mr. Ortega nodded. "Then I'll contact him."

"Can I ask why Alex doesn't want her family to know she is alive?" Jaxson asked. "Mr. Coronado looks like he hasn't slept in days—at least that's what Glinda said."

"Someone tried to kill Alex, and she doesn't know who. I told her not to trust anyone. And I mean anyone—except me, of course."

I expected him to flash us a smile, but he did not.

"How does staying dead help find the killer?" Jaxson asked.

"Alex thinks the killer will slip up and show his true colors. That, and she wants to remain alive. She might not be as well prepared for a second attack."

"How did Alex escape?" Rihanna asked.

"I'll give you the short story. She suspected someone wanted her out of the way. And no, she doesn't know who, but there have been signs. Suffice it to say, she figured when she was underwater and vulnerable, it would give the killer a chance to attempt to murder her. She claimed she wanted to find out once and for all who was out to stop her. It was why she insisted that everyone go diving."

"She's lucky she wasn't stabbed instead of merely having her hose cut," I shot back.

"Alex was aware that could happen, so she wore protective gear under her suit."

"She thinks of everything." Or almost everything. She didn't think someone would steal her necklace.

"Alex also carried a small rebreather that she'd tucked away in her suit. It gave her about five minutes of air. Once her oxygen was compromised, she pressed an alarm on her signal watch. I, along with Chuck Abernathy—her dive instructor from way back—rescued her. That's why we were stationed nearby the caves in a small boat."

The pieces fell into place. "Nina said she spotted two people, but that you were off in the distance."

"Yes. We had an underwater scooter ready and waiting if Alex pressed the alarm. With her five-minute air supply, we needed to be able to reach her quickly."

That was a lot to take in. "Where is she now?"

"In a hotel in Palm Ridge."

Doubt began to creep in about whether Hugo was right about the necklace being a fake. "How about we tell Steve what happened, and then we can get the necklace?"

"Are you certain Gustavo returned it to the safe?" Jaxson asked. "He was a little upset to learn that we thought the necklace was a fake, which is why I figured he ran out of the Hex and Bones."

I had forgotten about that. "You're right. What do you think he'd do with it?"

"Steve was there. He saw Gustavo's reaction. Steve should have told him to return it as it might be evidence in a crime."

I sucked in a breath. "You're right. I think."

"Who is Steve?" Mr. Ortega asked.

"Sorry, he's our sheriff. He's looking into Alex's death."

"I see. Let's go talk with him. Alex needs that necklace."

Too bad she was going to be very disappointed. Since I wanted Rihanna to come with us in order to make sure this man was telling the truth, I invited her.

"You bet," she said.

Iggy looked up at me. "Don't even think about not taking me."

Neither Steve nor Mr. Ortega could understand Iggy, but he would be easier to deal with if I allowed him to join us.

"Hop in the purse, my little detective."

Iggy climbed in, and we left. Mr. Ortega kept a step or two behind us as we crossed the street. Being a bodyguard, he probably felt more comfortable in that position.

We entered the sheriff's department. While our supreme gossip queen was at the reception desk, Steve was standing over at Nash's desk showing the deputy something on his infamous yellow notepad. He looked up with a combination of surprise and maybe frustration that I had returned. And yes, I was getting good at reading his deadpan look.

"May we talk to you, Steve? It's about Alex's case." I wanted to imply Alex was still dead. No telling what Pearl would say if she knew the truth.

"Sure. Let's sit in the conference room." He turned to Nash. "Want to join us?"

"Of course."

Once we were seated around the table, Steve turned to me. "Tell me what's going on."

I motioned for Mr. Ortega to begin.

"I'm Geraldo Ortega, Alex Coronado's bodyguard. I'm here because I need to retrieve Alex's pink pearl necklace. And no, it's not my style. It's because Alex isn't dead."

Boom! Take that, Steve.

Chapter Eleven

"Excuse me?" Steve said.

I kept quiet. Alex's bodyguard knew the details better.

"Alex's dive instructor and I were close to the caves when someone cut Alex's air hose. We rescued her."

He certainly left out a lot of details, but Steve could ask for clarification if he wanted to.

"Was it a coincidence that you were close by?" our sheriff asked.

"No. Alex suspected someone might try to harm her."

"Had there been an attempt on her life before?" I asked. Steve stiffened, and I smiled sweetly. "Sorry, I couldn't help myself."

For a split second, I thought he might smile. He did not.

"Go on, Mr. Ortega," the sheriff said.

"Alex was in a near car crash recently."

"Was anyone hurt?" he asked.

"No, thankfully. I was driving and managed to avoid the other vehicle. The car, whose driver I don't know, was coming toward us. At the last minute, he swerved into our lane. I was lucky that no one was on the sidewalk when I drove up on it."

"Did you report the incident?" Nash asked.

"Yes, but nothing came of it. Yet. It was dark, and they had their high beams on. I described the car the best I could."

One incident wouldn't warrant all that concern. Or would it?

"Anything else?" Steve asked.

"I'm not saying that Ricardo Coronado is connected to his wife's death in any way, but he wasn't happy that Alex wanted to merge their company with another. It would mean he had less say so in the running of the business."

"But it's Alex's company, not his." Okay, once more I couldn't help myself for mentioning that fact.

"You're right, which is why she felt justified in making the deal."

"What about Gustavo? Was he upset, too?" I was curious if Mr. Ortega's opinion of Alex's son matched what Nina said about him.

"I try to stay out of the everyday comings and goings, but it is my job to notice any hostile attitude toward my client."

"Gustavo was hostile toward his mother?" Steve asked.

"Not directly. He often is looking to please his father, so if Ricardo was upset, Gustavo was, too. My opinion is that Gustavo doesn't have the desire to think on his own."

Ouch. "What about Nina?"

His brows rose. "She's new and seems very attentive to all of Alex's wishes. She isn't a threat."

It was always the ones you didn't suspect who often were guilty. "Why hasn't Alex told her devoted assistant that she's alive? Alex must know that her death would upset Nina."

He nodded. "I advised her not to tell anyone. I suppose it is a blessing that Alex's parents have passed. Otherwise, her death would have destroyed them."

Nash placed his elbows on the table. "Her husband seemed quite upset. If he had nothing to do with her death, it is cruel not to tell him. Which makes me feel Alex suspects him."

"Alex Coronado is a savvy businesswoman. She is right to suspect everyone, but she knows that if she is declared dead, the company's control goes to Ricardo."

"Would Gustavo benefit from her death?" I asked.

"Not according to her will, but Ricardo could, and probably would, promote his son."

"And the lawyer?" Steve placed his pen to his yellow pad, ready to take notes.

"Dante Diaz is a smart lawyer who Alex paid a premium to get. He won't lose any sleep over having to find another job."

"You don't think he might have a hidden agenda from a competitor?" Nash asked.

"I couldn't say. Alex would be better able to answer that."

From the way Mr. Ortega glanced at his watch, Alex's necklace was needed. Now. "Steve, is there any way we can get a hold of Alex's pearl necklace? She really needs it. She never told me the details, but it's a health related thing."

"What kind of health thing?" Steve asked Alex's bodyguard.

"Sir, I have no idea. And that is the truth."

I glanced over at Rihanna. She could read a person better than anyone. She looked over at me and winked, implying Mr. Ortega was telling the truth.

"Let me see what I can do," Steve said. "Glinda, is the safe still open?"

"I don't know, but Mr. Ortega has the code."

Steve huffed out a chuckle. "That would have saved us some time if we'd had that before."

"True, but then someone—read the killer—would know that Alex was still alive," I said.

"Touché."

"Do you all want to wait here while I get the necklace?" Steve looked around as he pushed back his chair.

"I have nothing else to do, sir."

"How about we go across the street and grab some breakfast?" I was really hungry.

"You three go," Mr. Ortega said. "I want to call Alex and give her an update."

From his tone, he was serious. "Okay." I pulled out my phone. "Let's exchange contact info."

As soon as we entered each other's number, Jaxson, Rihanna, Iggy, and I headed out to the Tiki Hut Grill. Thankfully, Pearl happened to be absent from the front desk at the moment, so I didn't have to make up a story to tell her.

Without saying a word, the four of us crossed the street. Once we entered the restaurant and found a seat, I placed my bag on the floor. I figured Iggy would do his thing. I couldn't blame him for not wanting to stay cooped up in a bag for the next hour.

Iggy stuck out his head. "I'm going to take a stroll on the beach."

"What? You don't normally do that. What gives?"

"I've had this need to get out and breathe the fresh air since the storm hit."

I studied my iguana to make sure someone hadn't switched him out for another of his kind, even though I believed he was unique. Iggy never talked like that. Maybe Hugo and Genevieve had been filling his head with stuff like this. "Okay."

Jaxson pushed back his chair. "I'll carry you out there, buddy. Navigating through all these people could be a problem."

"You are the best," my little familiar said mimicking what I always said to Jaxson.

"Be right back," Jaxson said.

I turned to Rihanna. "Did you detect any deceit in what Alex's bodyguard said?"

"No. None. He was genuinely concerned about his boss."

"If Alex asked him and her dive instructor to come down to Florida and stand by in case of trouble, she must trust them completely."

"I would assume so."

My cousin might only be nineteen, but she was incredibly insightful. "Do you have any idea who might have taken the necklace, or who tried to kill Alex for that matter?"

She smiled. "You haven't given me the Glinda Goodall run down with the white board yet. I haven't been around much, remember?"

"Yes, I know, but you seem to know stuff." I wish I had her abilities. "I've really missed your input."

She reached across the table and squeezed my hand. "As soon as you talk with Alex, you have to insist she tell you everything about the necklace. It will be the only way to find out the truth. And that's my input for the day."

I nodded. "You are right."

A few moments later, Jaxson returned from the beach just as Penny walked up to our table. "Hey, guys. What's up?" She held up a hand. "Don't tell me. You're working the vitamin heiress case."

I wanted to tell her that Alex was alive, but she might let something slip and ruin things. "We are. And we are also kind of in a hurry. We're waiting for Steve to get back to us about something, so we'll order now." I smiled, hoping she wouldn't question anything.

The problem with my good friend was that Penny was not only a witch, she could detect a lie as fast as Rihanna could. Penny couldn't read minds exactly, but she somehow knew when a person wasn't telling the truth. Had she been wrong before? Yes, but not often.

"I get it. It's secret spy stuff. You know that if you need any help, you can call me."

This time I smiled for real. "You got it."

"What do you all want?"

We each ordered our usual, and Penny left to deliver our requests to the chef.

"Where did Iggy want to go?" I asked Jaxson.

"I put him next to some sea oats. I think he was trying to hide while he kept an eye out for Tippy."

"What happened to the petition?" Rihanna asked.

I guess we hadn't told her. "Iggy decided not to turn it in. Aunt Fern convinced him that it's bad to upset the balance of nature. Without seagulls, rats would take their place."

She scrunched up her face. "Is that true?"

"I checked," Jaxson said. "And it is true."

"Maybe we should feed Tippy and his friends. I'd rather have seagulls than rats," Rihanna said.

"Amen to that," I said.

Less than ten minutes later, Penny returned with our meals. "Enjoy."

"Thanks."

It wouldn't take Steve long to find out about the necklace since I imagine the family would turn it over right away. If they didn't, they'd look guilty. The question was whether Steve would end up with the real one or the fake one.

Since time was of the essence, we quickly ate, paid, and then returned to the sheriff's office. Pearl was once again seated in her spot.

"Is Steve back?" I asked before looking around.

She nodded behind her. "He came in a bit ago."

Sure enough, Steve was in the conference room with Alex's bodyguard and Nash. "Thanks."

It was just the three of us who headed to the back to join them since Iggy hadn't returned from his beach surveillance. As soon as I stepped in, I spotted the pink necklace. "You got it!"

"It wasn't hard," Steve said. "The son had it, and he turned it over."

"What did you tell him as to why you needed it?"

"I told him I needed it as part of the investigation, which was true. I should have asked him to leave it with me after that location spell, but I was off my game at the moment. Magic does that to me sometimes."

"I see." I faced Mr. Ortega. "Now what?"

"I was waiting for you to return. I know Alex wants to

speak with you."

My face flushed. "That's great. I hope the invitation extends to my two coworkers."

"If you trust them, then I trust them."

"How about we follow you to the motel? That way you don't have to come back here," Jaxson suggested.

"Sounds good." Alex's bodyguard turned to Steve. "Thank you."

"Of course. Please inform Mrs. Coronado that I will have to confer with her at some point. I am happy to drive to Palm Ridge if she doesn't want to come here."

"I will let her know."

With the necklace in hand, we left. Mr. Ortega had parked in front of our office, which made it convenient. While we doubted anyone would notice that we were with the bodyguard on the way to visit Alex, we decided to meet him there.

"It's the Palm Ridge Motel," he said. "Do you know where that is?" Mr. Ortega asked Jaxson.

"Yes. What's her room number?"

"She's in room 203."

We told him we'd wait a few minutes before leaving. I typed the information into my phone since I often forgot details. Once the three of us trudged up the stairs, we entered our office, and who should be there but Iggy! Unfortunately, the side of his body was a bit swollen.

"Iggy, what happened?"

He crawled over to me. "I got bit."

My heart was crushed. I squatted down and picked him up in order to inspect the irritated site. "Who bit you? Not

Tippy, I hope."

"I don't think seagulls have teeth. It was a crab. A really big, mean looking crab."

Seagulls could bite, but I wasn't about to mention that to Iggy. As for the crab, most likely Iggy had seen one crawl out of its hole and decided to investigate the newcomer to the beach. "I'm sorry. Does it itch?"

"Can seagulls fly? Or maybe I should say, do seagulls poop?"

"How about I put some anti-itch cream on it?" Of course, I had no idea if that would have any effect on an iguana's body. I turned to Jaxson. "Do you think you can look up the effect of a crab bite on an iguana?"

"Seriously? I know the Internet is vast, but I'm not sure it will address this issue. But... I will look."

I really didn't think he'd find anything either.

About a minute later, he spun around in his chair. "All I found is what to do if a crab bites you. They say to flush it with water and clean it. That's all. But crabs only grab onto you when they feel threatened. If you panic, they hold on tighter since they think they will fall off."

I looked over at Iggy. "What do you have to say for yourself, young man. Did you tease this crab?"

"It wasn't my fault. He jumped on my back and started to crawl around."

I shook my head. "You are so much bigger than he is. You could have rolled over. He would have dislodged himself and gone his own way."

"I spotted Tippy, and I wanted to make sure he kept away from our plants. I didn't have time to think."

"Uh-huh. We have to go, but let me wash the wound so it doesn't get infected." Assuming it could. I didn't know all that much about iguana anatomy since I never had the occasion to speak with a vet about him. I couldn't remember when Iggy had been ill.

As quickly as I could, I washed off the sand and tended to the wound. It looked superficial at best.

"What if I blow up?" he asked.

"You mean if you have an allergic reaction?"

"Yes."

"Go downstairs and show Drake. While you can't communicate with him, if he sees your condition, he'll know what to do." Jaxson's brother was always level-headed.

Iggy tilted his head to the side a bit more so that he was looking me directly in the eye. "Are you sure?"

"Yes." I tried to sound very confident.

"Okay. Where are you guys going?"

"To speak with Alex."

"Tell her hi for me."

I smiled. "I will."

The three of us took the staircase down to the parking lot, and I couldn't wait to hear the truth about the necklace.

Chapter Twelve

I'LL ADMIT I was worried for a minute that maybe Alex wasn't alive and that the man who claimed to be her bodyguard was just a gold digger. He could have spotted her pink pearl necklace and thought he could sell it for a goodly amount. Had Rihanna not been with us and vouched for him, I might have been more hesitant to go to this motel.

Even after we pulled into the parking lot, I had to paint on a smile as I slipped out of the car.

"What room did he say Alex was in?" Jaxson asked.

"Room 203."

He studied the two-story motel. "This doesn't seem like a place a rich heiress would stay in."

"Maybe that's why she picked it." I thought it was a brilliant cover.

One of the doors on the second floor opened, and Geraldo Ortega stepped out. He motioned we come up.

"Let's do this," Jaxson said.

As we neared her room, Alex poked her head out for a second, and when she waved, my muscles relaxed. "She's really alive!" I whispered.

Mr. Ortega motioned us inside the small, dingy room. Alex was dressed in ill-fitting jeans and an overly large shirt.

But that didn't matter. She was alive. Since her hose had been cut, all she would have had on was her bathing suit and wet suit. I bet Mr. Ortega did the clothes shopping.

I realized it might not be proper, but I couldn't help but hug her. "I'm so happy you're alive."

We stepped away from each other at the same time. "That makes two of us."

When Alex looked over at Rihanna, I introduced her. "My cousin is also a witch. Actually, she's very talented in knowing if a person has lied." Saying she could often read minds might creep Alex out.

She stuck out her hand. "Nice to meet you, and I must say, what a great talent to have." Alex waved a hand to show the size of the room. "There isn't much space, but find a seat where you can. I'm sure you have a lot of questions for me."

"Yes." I took out the fake necklace from my purse. "Hugo said this is not the original, but I'll let you decide." It's possible the real one was switched back.

Her eyes widened. Alex took the necklace and clasped it to her neck. "I'm so glad it's back. You have no idea how much I need this."

"So this is the real one?"

She stilled and then studied it. "I really can't say until I find out if it works."

"I think it would be good if you told us what this necklace can do." I honestly didn't say that to be nosy. If this one was a fake, we needed to know what was really at stake here. A lot of things could affect her health.

"I'll tell you what I know," Alex said. "As I mentioned, this was a gift from my mother. If I wear it four hours a day, it slows down the aging process."

I sucked in a breath and then glanced over at Jaxson and Rihanna. Jaxson's chin was tucked in as if he, too, found her claim preposterous. If it weren't for the fact that she looked more like her son's sister than his mother, I might have laughed.

Rihanna was focused intently on Alex. "What happens if you don't wear it? Will you age normally?" Rihanna asked.

"I'm afraid not. The aging is accelerated, which was why I was so desperate to have the necklace back. I've already noticed many lines on my face since yesterday. I will eventually look older than fifty-four. Sad to say, my company relies on my image."

"I totally understand. No one wants the head of a vitamin company to look bad." I hope that wasn't a tacky thing to say.

Alex clasped the necklace and then stilled for a moment. "You might be right."

The slack jaw and wide eyes almost scared me. "About what? That the necklace could be a fake?"

"Yes."

That stunk. "How can you tell?"

She let out a breath. "It's hard to explain. When you found this before, I was so relieved that I put it on but failed to pay attention to the slight vibration that I normally feel when it touches my skin."

"You're sure it's a replica then?" Jaxson asked.

"Sadly, yes, and we need to find the real one." She removed it and placed it on the small table next to her.

"That's easier said than done. Any suggestions on how we do that?"

Her shoulders drooped. "No."

"If someone went to the trouble of making a replica, it wasn't an ordinary thief," Jaxson said.

Alex sat up straighter. "You're right. That implies it was either my husband, son, assistant, or our legal counsel."

"Could someone else have arrived in town that you don't know about—like someone who wants to ruin your company? A competitor maybe?"

She let out a breath. "Gustavo's wife came here afterward. You met her, but you're right. I suppose another small vitamin company could have sent down a spy, since they wouldn't want me to merge with a bigger firm. Doing so would create more competition for them. Here's the thing. So far, no one has even approached me about another offer. I'm not sure many companies know about the merger."

"Someone from the larger company could have leaked the information."

"They could have." Her slackened jaw indicated the enormity of this situation.

"You suspected someone wanted to harm you, right?" I wanted to confirm her bodyguard's story.

"Yes."

"Alex, I told them about the near car accident we were involved in," Mr. Ortega said.

She nodded. "I also received some messages saying if I went ahead with the merger that I would be sorry."

"Who sent them?" I asked.

Alex huffed. "We couldn't trace them. It was sent by some burner phone."

"You didn't recognize the wording as that of someone you

knew?" I asked.

"No." She stood, walked over to her purse, and pulled out her phone. She scrolled through some messages. "Here is one of them."

I motioned that she give it to Jaxson. "He's the tech expert."

"I hope you can figure it out."

Jaxson read it. "I'll have to take this with me to see if I can do a search for the sender."

"Be my guest."

"Alex?" Rihanna asked.

"Yes?"

"If someone in your group took the necklace, he or she would have done so in order to wear it, right? Or maybe they needed to sell it."

"I don't think the pearls are worth much. It's the spell that was put on them that makes the necklace valuable. Selling it doesn't make much sense."

"Who have you told about its powers?" Rihanna asked. "Mr. Ortega, for example, wouldn't have taken it, because he didn't know what it could do."

Mr. Ortega huffed out a laugh. "I might not know much about fashion, but I would have assumed that the necklace would bring a lot of money. Alex is a wealthy heiress. Most would think that everything she wears is valuable." Mr. Ortega held up a hand. "But I did not take it, I assure you."

She smiled. "I'm sure you didn't. As for who knew about its powers, only my husband and son were aware of its ability. No one else."

Or so she believed. He probably told his wife.

"Technically, all we'd have to do then is wait a while to see who doesn't age or who starts to look younger, and we'll have our thief," Rihanna said.

Alex tilted her head. "I guess, but I'm the only person who has ever worn it. I couldn't tell you how long the age reduction process takes. I've had it for over ten years."

"Didn't your husband ever want to give it a try? I know men don't wear pink pearl necklaces, but to keep from aging I would think he'd give it a go and wear it to bed," I said.

"He asked about it, but I told him that since he wasn't a warlock, it wouldn't work." She glanced off to the side. "Though I don't know why I thought that. My mother never gave me the details of the necklace before she passed."

"You never asked her about it?" Perhaps her own mother didn't know, since it had been passed down to her from her mother, Alex's grandmother.

"No. I was so upset over her impending death that I wasn't thinking about my own health or my looks."

The necklace was clearly special. There had to be something we were missing. "Would your mother know?"

"Probably, but like I said, she's passed."

I glanced over at Rihanna and hoped she would read my mind.

"We could do a séance." Rihanna sounded youthfully upbeat.

"A séance? As in you want to talk to my mother? Do those things actually work?"

Alex wasn't a practicing witch, so I understood her skepticism. "They often do, but since I don't see any candles here, someone would have to buy some."

"I can send Geraldo out to get what you need. I'd rather not be seen."

"I can understand that." I explained how many we'd need and their size. Palm Ridge wasn't a large town, so it shouldn't take him long to purchase them.

As soon as he left, I went over with her what to expect from a séance.

"It's possible your mother will speak through you. We'll record what you say since you may not remember much. Or she can appear as a ghost. Both Rihanna and I can see ghosts, but they often come quickly and leave even faster, so we should go over what you want to ask her."

For the next fifteen minutes, Alex penned her questions and then numbered them in order from most important to least important since time was of the essence. Just as she finished, her bodyguard returned with the needed items.

"Here is what you requested." He handed me the bag.

"Thank you, Geraldo."

He returned outside, probably to keep watch. I couldn't imagine Mr. Ortega would be creeped out by a ghost. Standing outside a hotel door screamed that someone inside was important, but who was I to judge?

"Where would you like these set up?" Alex asked.

"The table is perfect." I looked inside the bag. He'd done a good job finding the right size.

Now I wish I had Iggy with me. He was the one who often sensed when a ghost was near, mainly because he cheated and opened his eyes.

Rihanna and I made short order of setting out the candles. "If you would please sit here, Alex." I looked over at Jaxson.

"You, too. You aren't getting out of this."

Jaxson had been involved in several séances and knew the routine. The shades were drawn, so the room was quite dim already.

I lit the candles. "Place your hands like so and make sure that your fingers are touching the person next to you. Don't break the contact or the connection with the spirit world will be lost. And keep your eyes closed."

"How will you know if my mom's ghost appears?"

If I had Iggy with me, he'd signal me, but he wasn't here. "I'll know." I hoped.

There was one flaw in my logic. How was I to read the questions to ask Alex's mom if my eyes were closed? I guess I'd have to cheat a little. I opened my eyes, read the first question, and then closed them again.

"Mrs. Hammond, your daughter Alex really needs your help. Someone stole her magical pearl necklace that you gave her, and we need to know what happens if the thief wears the necklace? Will it do what it did for Alex?"

That was actually two questions, but I might only get one shot. Then we waited. The soft whooshing of cars driving by were interrupted by a few hotels doors closing. Busy place.

"Alex?" The faint sound of a far off voice floated by. I had to open my eyes.

I immediately squeezed Rihanna's hand to indicate Alex's mother was there.

"Mrs. Hammond, what can you tell us about the powers surrounding the necklace?" I asked.

"No one but Alex can wear it, unless she passes. If someone else wears it, he or she will be harmed."

That sounded ominous. "In what way?"

The candles went out. And then the ghost disappeared. Oh, come on. Was it something I said that made her leave so quickly? Or didn't I know how to do a proper séance? Most likely she was a ghost who was only able to stay for a short while. I thought I'd get the chance to ask a couple of questions at least.

If Alex's mom had been a witch, she might have had to earn credits to stay longer—or were credits needed only when a person wasn't called forth in a séance? The one chance I had to interrogate some other ghosts about this very topic, they hadn't stayed around long enough to answer all of my concerns. Darn.

I exhaled and released my hold. "She's gone." I looked over at Rihanna. "Did you hear her?"

"Yes, but I didn't cheat by opening my eyes."

I wasn't sure it mattered in this case.

"I didn't hear her. Why was that?" Alex asked.

"I have no idea. I'm sorry." That was strange, especially since Alex was a witch.

"How did my mother sound?"

Sound? I really hadn't paid attention to whether she was happy or sad. "She only stayed for a few seconds. What she said was that if someone wears your necklace, they will be harmed."

Alex sucked in a breath. "Harmed how?"

"That I don't know. I asked, but she left before answering."

Alex slumped in her seat. "That didn't help us much, did it?"

"This might be wishful thinking on my part, but I think people who return use their words wisely."

"Meaning?"

"Your mom might have been giving us a clue. I'm not saying that the person who took your necklace is the same one who tried to harm you, but if we find the real necklace, we might be closer to finding the killer." I hoped I wasn't making that up, nor could I pinpoint what her mom said that led me to that conclusion. A sixth sense perhaps?

Someone knocked on the motel door, causing me to jump. Just as Alex started to get up, Mr. Ortega came in and closed the door behind him.

"I think we've been found."

Chapter Thirteen

"SOMEONE KNOWS I'M here?" Alex sounded scared—really scared. "Who is it?"

"I don't know," Mr. Ortega said. "I could be wrong, but the same white crossover SUV has been driving back and forth a few times."

"What kind of car did you drive down here, Alex?" Jaxson asked.

"A black Ford Escalade."

"It wasn't a family member then," I mumbled.

"They could have rented a car," Rihanna tossed in.

Or it could have been nothing, and Alex's bodyguard was a little paranoid.

"We need to leave," Mr. Ortega stated with quite a bit of urgency.

"And go where? I can't return to Atlanta."

There had to be a safe place for her.

"You could stay at the office," Rihanna offered. She looked over at me. "I could sleep on your couch, Glinda."

"Or Alex and Mr. Ortega could stay at my two-bedroom place," Jaxson said. "I could sleep on Glinda's sofa."

It might be time to buy that pull out sofa I've been wanting. "What do you think, Alex? It's your call."

"Are you and Jaxson still planning to work on this case?"

"Of course." I glanced to Jaxson to make certain he was on board. Thankfully, he nodded.

"Is your place in town, Jaxson?" she asked.

"No. It's in a quiet neighborhood."

"Then could I stay at the office? I'd feel safer being across the street from the sheriff's department. Geraldo said it's not that big, but I could buy a cot for him. I feel safer having him there."

"Sure. We need a cot anyway."

Rihanna waved a hand. "Alex and I are about the same height with the same darkish hair. If I could borrow one of Alex's hats, I could have Mr. Ortega drive me to Jaxson's house. If anyone follows, they'd think Alex was staying there." She faced Jaxson. "But if we do this, could you grab some of my clothes before you go over to Glinda's for the night?"

"Absolutely. I'll need to pick up some things for myself, too."

I had a really smart cousin.

"I like the bait and switch," Alex said, sounding much calmer.

While she packed, we went over the logistics again. Alex would go to the office with me and Jaxson. It would be fairly easy to have her enter through the beachside back entrance and then come up the inside staircase. Hopefully, she wouldn't have to stay too many days. Not being able to leave would be difficult mentally, but it would be a lot safer than showing her face.

After lending Rihanna a hat, Alex gathered her few belongings. Mr. Ortega then checked them out of the motel.

Jaxson drove Alex and me back to the office while Rihanna went with the bodyguard to Jaxson's place. Alex didn't say much on the way to Witch's Cove, and I couldn't blame her. Not having her necklace would be a terrible blow to her since she'd age rapidly.

Once in front of our office, Jaxson parked. "Alex and I will go around to the back," I said.

"I'll carry up your suitcase," he said, "but first I want to make sure we weren't followed."

It was a good idea to split up. Knowing the way Jaxson's mind worked, he'd probably pretend to do something on his truck in order to watch for a white SUV driving back and forth.

As we headed down the alley to the back of our office, Alex kept her head lowered until we entered through the rear entrance to the wine and cheese shop.

"I'll be right with you," Drake called from the front. I'd forgotten about that noisy door chime.

"It's only me," I called out.

"You aren't an *only*, Glinda."

Was Jaxson's brother not the best too? He stepped into the back and stopped when he spotted Alex. He hadn't met her, but maybe Jaxson had let him know that she was alive, but why would he? Or rather when would he have told Drake?

He held out his hand. "I'm Drake Harrison, Jaxson's better looking brother."

She smiled. "I'm..."

"This is Alex, the woman your good friend Dave thinks he let drown."

His mouth dropped open. "You're alive? How is that

possible? Or are you a fish witch?"

I had no idea what a fish witch was, but maybe he thought it could be a person who could breathe underwater. I called those people free divers.

"It's a long story, and we can't have anyone know she is alive—not even Dave. At least not yet. Steve knows, but that's all." I waved a hand. "Okay, Rihanna, Jaxson, Iggy, and Alex's bodyguard know as well."

Drake held up both hands, acting a bit confused. "Why are you here?"

"Alex is going to hide out upstairs until we get things cleared up."

"And Andorra? Does she know?" Drake asked.

I looked over at Alex to see if she had a problem with Drake's girlfriend finding out. Most likely we'd have to use her talents, and that of her familiar, at some point.

"Not yet, but can we wait to tell her?" Alex said. "I need to figure things out first."

"Sure. Just tell me when." The bell at the front of the store rang, signaling a customer. "I gotta go, but you know where I am if you need anything."

"Thanks." Drake was such a wonderful guy.

Once I led Alex upstairs, who should be standing in the middle of the office area but Iggy himself.

"About time you got here. I thought that Alex was hiding out at a motel or something." My familiar gave her the once over, but I couldn't quite tell what he was thinking.

"Change of plans, but you can't say anything to anyone about her being alive," I warned.

"Me? Who would I tell? Tippy?"

"You might mention it to Aunt Fern or Aimee." Oh no. I don't think I told him not to say anything. "You haven't said anything yet, have you?"

"No, but only because I haven't seen them."

"That's good." I picked him up to check out the side of his body for any further reaction from his little beach incident. "How is the crab bite?"

"It's okay, but I think I'll keep away from them from now on. They're mean."

"Lots of animals are mean if you provoke them. Otherwise, they can be nice." Sure, I made that up, but I thought it was true.

"Whatever."

I set him down, and then turned to Alex. "You can take Rihanna's room." My cousin was obsessively neat, so her room would be picked up. "I'll grab a set of clean sheets for you."

"Just tell me where they are, and I'll change the bed."

Alex seemed to need to keep busy. "In the closet next to the bathroom."

"I'll get settled and be right out."

I left her to do her thing. The front door opened, and Jaxson came in, carrying a bag with Alex's things in it. "What were you doing outside for so long?"

"I was outside for a max of ten minutes, but I was pretending to work on the truck. I didn't see a white SUV drive by more than once."

"Maybe our ruse worked."

"Let's hope." He nodded toward the back room. "How is she?" Jaxson kept his voice to a whisper.

I shrugged. "She's getting settled—or she will be as soon

as she has her stuff."

"I'll give it to her."

"By the way, we ran into your brother."

Jaxson's brows rose. "You told him who Alex was?"

"I didn't want to lie, but I asked him not to say anything to anyone. If his friend Dave calls him again, it will be hard to keep that information secret, though."

"No kidding. I'm fixing a cup of coffee. Want anything?" Jaxson asked.

"I'd love a tea."

"I'll see if Alex wants something, too."

With Alex's bag in hand, Jaxson slipped into the small kitchen. Before he returned, someone knocked on the front door, and I rushed to answer it. "Mr. Ortega. Come in."

He was hauling a box that appeared to contain an air mattress. I suppose if he'd purchased a foldaway cot and someone spotted him, it would be a bit obvious that we had a guest. Besides, finding an air mattress was easy in this town. A cot? Not so much.

"How's Alex?" he asked as he set down the box.

"She's getting settled."

I heard Jaxson knock on the bedroom door and then ask her if she wanted something to drink. I assumed he was delivering her the bag of clothes, too.

A moment later, Jaxson came out with a mug of coffee for himself and a tea for me. "Geraldo. Anyone follow you to my house?"

"I spotted the white SUV a few times."

I didn't like it and spun to face Jaxson. "While I'm happy that they fell for the switch, what if this person is the killer?

He might break into your house if he thinks Rihanna is Alex. He could try to kill her—in her sleep. I should have insisted she sleep on my coach." The horror had the bile in my stomach coming up. Why hadn't I thought of that sooner?

Jaxson set down his coffee and placed a hand on my arm. "Rihanna is resourceful, but I better make sure she's okay. Let me grab some of her things first and then head over there."

"I'll do it since Alex is in the bedroom."

"Sure."

I knocked on Rihanna's door, and then explained that I needed to pick up a few of her things.

"Of course."

I found her suitcase in the closet and filled it with a few days' worth of clothes.

"Did I hear Geraldo?"

"Yes. He's pretty sure someone followed them, so Jaxson is going to make sure Rihanna is safe."

"I am so sorry to bring this mess to you, but I had no one I could trust."

I gave her my best smile. "Not a problem."

It wasn't the first time we'd been in the presence of a killer, and it wouldn't be the last. Once I finished gathering everything, I returned to the main room and handed Rihanna's bag to Jaxson. "Are you coming back tonight?"

"I don't think that's a good idea."

I nodded. "Two places, two bodyguards. Check."

"Three bodyguards." Iggy came out from under the sofa.

I looked down at him. "You're going to protect me when I go back to the apartment?"

"Yes. If anyone comes in, I can cloak myself, climb up his

body, and bite him."

I gave him my most serious expression. "That would surely scare him. Thank you."

"You bet."

Jaxson swallowed a smile, leaned over, and kissed me quickly. "Call if anything strange happens."

"I'll be fine. Take care of my cousin."

He grabbed his mug of coffee and left. "Can I get you something to drink?" I asked Mr. Ortega.

"I'm good."

Alex was stepping out of the bedroom when heavy footsteps pounded up the back staircase, and I froze. That wasn't Drake. I'd know his sound anywhere.

Dave Sanders rounded the corner. "Is it true?" His voice nearly cracked.

Before I could answer, a second set of footsteps shot up the stairs. Now that would be Drake.

"Sorry, Glinda. I had to tell him."

If Penny had been involved in something tragic like this, I would have caved too. "I understand."

Since Alex was right there, there was no reason for me to explain.

"Hello, Dave. I am so sorry about the confusion," Alex said.

"Confusion? Is this some sort of joke on your part?" When he took a step forward, Mr. Ortega was in his face in a second.

"Calm down. Someone tried to kill her. She had to lay low." Ortega's voice came out a growl.

It was as if the bodyguard had poked a hole in Dave, who

then stepped back and stabbed a hand through his disheveled hair. "I'm sorry. Of course. Even though I found the cut hose, I forgot that meant someone wanted her dead." He turned to Alex. "Why didn't you tell me you were alive, though? I've been worried sick."

He was a smart guy. He'd figure it out. I waited a beat, but a second later my patience ran out, and I had to ask. "Why do you think?"

His mouth opened slightly. "You think this person will try again?"

"Yes." Alex answered for me. "I am so sorry, but I needed everyone to truly believe he'd succeeded in killing me."

It was a little awkward with everyone standing. "Let's all take a seat, and Alex can tell you everything, Dave."

"Thanks. I kind of want to hug you, but after my outburst, I don't think it would be appropriate."

She flashed Dave a quick smile, stepped forward, and gave him a brief embrace. "Please sit. I do owe you an apology."

Once we were seated, Alex went through the series of events once more.

"Where did the attack happen? I found your tank near the exit of the cave," Dave said.

"I was close to there," she said. "I'm glad you found the equipment. Swimming with it would have slowed me down."

"I get it. This implies the person who attacked you could have entered the cave—or rather the tunnel—from either end."

"I figured that, too," Alex said.

"I trust you never saw this person?" I asked.

Alex dipped her head. "No. I was examining the beautiful

stone on the walls and wasn't paying attention. It's my fault for allowing myself to become distracted. I should have been more attentive. After all, I'd hired Geraldo and Clark in case something like this happened. Coming after me while I was underwater when I was the most vulnerable made sense. The trip down here had been uneventful until my necklace went missing. I guess my focus was on the theft and not on who might want to harm me."

"Do you think you might be up for discussing who you believe cut your hose?" Having the actual victim present would be so beneficial.

"If I want to learn who did this, I need to do what I can."

"Thank you. Let me get my white board, and we can begin."

Chapter Fourteen

I CARRIED THE discussion board back into the main room and placed it where everyone could see it. I wasn't sure if Dave or Drake were up for staying, but they were welcome to join in.

"Everyone ready to brainstorm?" I tried to sound upbeat, despite my shaking hands. My worry over Rihanna being in possible danger wouldn't go away, but knowing Jaxson was with her helped.

"I'd love to stay and grace you with my deep intellect, but I need to get back to the store," Drake said. "Duty calls, you know."

I appreciated his attempt at levity. We could have used him. Drake, in particular, was better than most at putting clues together. "I know you have a business to run. Go."

"Mind if I stay?" Dave asked. "I don't know Alex and her family well, but I know the area. I might be useful."

I smiled. "Absolutely." I turned to Alex's bodyguard. "Where is this dive instructor Alex hired?"

"Clark returned home. His continued presence might look suspicious."

"I see. Thanks for clarifying."

Okay. Time for business. It might be a little awkward to

show Alex our thoughts and possible suspects, but hopefully, she would correct any misconceptions and not hold them against us.

"If it's not too late, we should ask the sheriff to join us," Mr. Ortega suggested. "He said he wanted to speak with Alex. It is his case, after all."

Why hadn't I thought of that? I had been thrown off my game ever since I learned Alex was still alive. "Great idea. I'll call him to see if he wants to come over now or wait until tomorrow to see what we've come up with." I pulled out my phone and stepped into the kitchen for a bit of privacy.

Steve answered on the second ring. "Glinda?"

"Yes. Alex is here with me at the office, and we are about to go over the possible suspects. Would you like to join us?"

"Are you kidding? I'll be right over." With that he disconnected. That was probably the fastest conversation I'd ever had with the man.

I tucked away my phone and returned to the main area. "Steve will be right over," I announced as I sat down.

Iggy crawled up next to me. "You might need my input," he announced.

I wasn't sure how he could help, but I was willing to have him there. I looked over at Mr. Ortega. "You probably noticed me talking to Iggy, but he talks back. Only those with magical powers can hear him."

"I see."

Hopefully, Alex had told him about familiars and how they were imbued with magic. Surely, she'd mentioned that I was a witch.

Alex stood, walked over to the white board, and studied

it. "You've been busy."

"It's only a beginning, trust me. I'm sure much of it is wrong."

"That's for sure. You put me down as the potential killer? Did you really think I'd try to kill myself?"

From her shocked and slightly angry voice, we'd misjudged her. "I wanted to be thorough and consider all possibilities. Murder or suicide is not always predictable."

Alex held out her palms. "You're right. You don't know me, and people do things like that all the time. I get it. I do. I had a friend who is now in jail for trying to scam her bank. She pretended she was dead, too, in order to avoid paying off a debt she owed."

That was sad. "What do you think of the other suspects?"

While Alex was reading the motives, Steve knocked and then came in. His gaze shot straight to her. "Her bodyguard was right. Alex is alive."

Did he think we'd made that up? I motioned to Steve to pull up the desk chair. No doubt he'd want to ask his own questions first. "Go ahead and ask away."

He nodded to Dave. "Thank you, Glinda. Alex, why did you do it?"

"Pretend to be dead?" Steve nodded. "I didn't like the alternative of dying." The sheriff's eyebrows rose. I guess he didn't appreciate her sarcasm.

"I understand," he finally said.

"Look, I didn't tell anyone I'd survived, because I feared this person wouldn't stop trying to kill me if he knew I'd lived. The next time, I might not be so lucky. I think Geraldo explained about the near car wreck?"

"He did."

"And Jaxson said he would try to trace the emails."

"I wouldn't be surprised if he looks into them tonight," I said.

Steve jotted something down in his notebook. "Do you have any thoughts as to who might have cut your hose?"

"I honestly don't know. The person came up behind me, and with a quick and decisive slice, cut my hose in half. It happened so fast that the sudden lack of oxygen took me by surprise. To say the least, I was a bit distracted." She explained about having her spare rebreather. "Once that was in my mouth, I turned around, but by then the person was a good twenty-feet away. Because the water was murky, I couldn't tell if it was a female or male."

"Thanks," he said.

Was that all he had to ask? Steve seemed too calm. I had imagined he and Nash had been working the case non-stop, even after Steve learned Alex was alive. "Do you know who it was, Steve?" I asked.

"No. My suspects are the same as yours, except that I added Jodi, the daughter-in-law."

I was thinking about her. "I figured she didn't take the necklace since she wasn't even in town, but I guess she could have cut Alex's hose." I did a mental count of those on the board. "She didn't go with you that day on the boat though, did she?"

"No. Jodi wasn't feeling well, and I suggested she stay at the hotel and rest," Alex explained.

"Is it possible that Jodi wasn't sick, and she hired a boat to take her out to the dive spot before you arrived?" I looked from Alex to Dave.

Dave shrugged. "I didn't see a third boat, but they could have come and gone."

I jotted down her name on the board. That would mean she was lying in wait for Alex. It would also mean she had a lot of air, possibly even carrying a spare tank. I knew very little about scuba diving and how long the air in the tanks lasted.

"Are we certain no one against the merger or against Alex herself was hiding in the caves, waiting for her?" Like Jodi might have been?

Alex bit down on her lip. "It's possible. We didn't make a secret of our destination. Even you knew that we were going diving."

"Have a possible name?" Steve asked.

"I wish I did," Alex said.

"Is there anyone in your company who would consider you to be an unfair boss? I'm not accusing you of anything, I'm just trying to think outside the box," Dave said.

She looked over at Mr. Ortega. "I guess a lot of people think I'm unreasonably strict, but if they had their way, nothing would get done."

"Tell me about it," Dave said. "Good help is hard to find."

Steve nodded to the board. "If you had to rank these people from most likely to have tried to kill you to the least, what ranking would you give each of them?"

Alex shook her head. "I can't even think like that. The betrayal would be too much. It's hard enough to know that I might have been blind to what my family was capable of, but clearly I have been."

I guess she lumped her assistant and the company lawyer into the family unit.

"Maybe we should concentrate on finding the necklace first," Steve said. "That might lead us to the killer. Or was the one we returned the real deal?"

"Sadly, it was not," Alex said.

I sat up straighter. "I have an idea."

"So do I," Iggy said as he crawled onto the coffee table.

I guess it was his turn to make some big announcement. "Yes, Iggy?"

"Let me interrogate everyone. I'll get the truth out of them."

What was he talking about? "Only Gustavo has any magical powers. The rest can't understand you."

He dropped down. "I forgot."

Poor Iggy. "But that actually leads me to my proposal, which is a slight variation of your suggestion."

He perked up. "What is it?"

"How about if Steve requests everyone on our list to go to his office? He then asks them if they know anything about the location of the real necklace. We'll discuss the murder attempt after that."

Steve's brows pinched. "No one is going to admit that they know anything about the necklace, nor are they going to admit they are guilty of murder—or attempted murder."

"True, but how about if we do a triple threat, assuming I can pull it off?"

He almost laughed. "What is a triple threat? Something you dreamed up? I don't think you mean you can sing, dance, and act."

"Hardly. I'll ask Penny and Rihanna to join me. They can tell if anyone is lying."

"Who's Penny?" Alex asked.

I explained that my friend was a witch who often could sense if a person was telling the truth. Same went for Rihanna. "That's where the spell comes in."

"Spell?" Steve asked.

I inhaled, wishing I'd thought this through a little better. "It won't be a real one, but the people won't know that."

"What are you claiming it can do?" Steve asked.

"I'll call it a truth spell. I'll need to come up with something fancy, like leaves floating in the air or fire shooting out of my fingertips. Yes, I know that is something only Genevieve can do, but I'll think of something unique. With enough fanfare, any non-magical person would be impressed. He might fear that I could do other bad things to him if he continues to lie. It might even cause him or her to confess."

"I've never seen you do anything like that before," Iggy said.

I translated what my sassy familiar said to Steve, Dave, and Mr. Ortega. "I know, which is why I might have to resort to using science rather than magic."

"Why not ask Hugo to help?" Iggy said. "He's made others tell the truth before."

"I know, but there are four people. Juggling all of them would be hard." Otherwise, I would ask him to help. The problem is that Steve would claim it was illegal.

"I'll bring in Jodi, too," Steve said. "She might offer up some useful information."

I had no problem with that. "Jodi can be like our control

group—or control person. We know she didn't take the necklace since she was still in Atlanta at the time of the theft." Or so Gustavo claimed.

"Sounds good," Steve said. "When will you be ready to do this little test?"

"I don't know if Penny works tomorrow, but even if she doesn't, I'll need time to find this magical spell that looks good but doesn't necessarily do anything."

"How about you call me as soon as you have a time?" he asked.

"Will do."

After a quick discussion about logistics, both Steve and Dave left—Steve by the front door and Dave by the interior staircase. Most likely he wanted to tell Drake all about what we'd discussed. We didn't really go over anyone's motive in detail, but we would at some point.

"It's late, and Iggy and I should be going too. Help yourself to what little food we have in the fridge. There is a convenience store on the edge of town that is open twenty-four hours, should you need anything."

I figured tomorrow Mr. Ortega would have to do takeout for Alex, since she couldn't be seen at any restaurant—especially in this busybody town.

"Thanks for everything, Glinda," Alex said.

I picked up Iggy. "I'll be trying to find that spell tomorrow, but call if you need me."

"You bet."

We left and went back to the apartment. I needed to call Jaxson to find out if he'd seen the white SUV on his drive back home.

Once inside, I placed Iggy on the floor and dropped down onto the sofa. Finally, I was able to relax and talk to him.

Jaxson answered right away. "Hey, what's up?"

I listened for any stress in his voice, but found none. Though that would be hard to tell in just three words.

"We had a slightly productive session. Steve came over."

"Really? That's great. Tell me about it."

I detailed everything we discussed. "In the end, I don't think anything new came of it."

"We've had hard cases before."

"I know. Did you have a chance to see who might have sent Alex those threatening emails?"

"I looked for a few minutes, but I haven't found anything. I don't have the right equipment at the house."

"Thanks for trying."

He chuckled. "I'm not giving up yet."

"I never thought you would. By the way, I had an idea, but it needs some work."

"I do love my pink lady's crazy schemes. Tell me."

I described what I'd figured out so far about the truth spell. "What do you think?" My fiancé was always the one to pop the bubble on my ideas.

"Honestly? I think it's our best chance of catching the thief and maybe even the attempted murderer."

I pumped a fist. "I'll give Levy a call now and set up a time to see him tomorrow."

"You do that. And Glinda?"

His voice had suddenly lowered. "Yes?"

"I love you."

I melted right into the sofa. "Back at you."

He chuckled. "The correct response is: I love you too."

Heat raced up my face. "I know, but Iggy is here."

"You realize that you can't use your familiar as an excuse forever, right?"

"I know." I inhaled. "I love you too," I whispered.

To my delight, bolts of lightning didn't light up the sky. Oh, wait. My necklace just flashed. That would be my grandmother. *Thank you, Nana.* I know she approved of my choice to marry the one and only Jaxson Harrison.

Chapter Fifteen

WHILE MY MEETING with Levy was earlier than I wanted, he was only free from nine to eleven the next morning. After my alarm went off at the crack of dawn, I got up, dressed, and then poured myself a cup of coffee.

Iggy waddled into the kitchen. "Did the apocalypse happen?"

"You know why I have to be up early. I'm going to see Levy. Do you want to come?"

He turned around and headed to the living room. "I don't do stupid questions this early in the morning."

I almost spit out my coffee. Iggy's level of sarcasm was growing rapidly. "Then get in my bag. I'll be right out."

I gulped down the rest of my drink, placed the cup in the sink, and fetched my purse and keys. Together, we went to the car.

Penny wasn't working today, so if I was able to find a spell and then learn how to do it, she'd be able to meet us at the sheriff's office when we needed her. Her ex-husband was picking up their son from school today, so my good friend would be available.

I'd already spoken with Rihanna, and she was on board for this charade too.

When we arrived at the library where the coven's books were housed, I parked and found Levy waiting for me at the entrance.

I lifted my bag. "Come on, Iggy. Let's see if we can pull this off."

"Maybe I can help with the spell."

"We'll see." I mentally scratched my head trying to remember if I'd ever seen him do a spell, but I couldn't recall.

I pushed open my car door and waved. "Thanks for always coming to my rescue." Levy never turned down my requests.

"Are you kidding? You challenge our coven in ways that no one ever has."

He was just being nice, but I appreciated it, nonetheless. After he used the eye and palm scanner to get into the super secure area, we walked down the narrow hallway to the room that housed the magic books.

"You remember Diego and Camila, right?"

I smiled. "Of course." I lifted Iggy out of my purse. "My familiar insisted on joining us."

"Iggy!" Camila said. "Come sit with me."

As fast as his little legs could carry him, he waddled over to her. She looked up at me and smiled. "He is so cool. I wish I had a pink iguana."

"He's one of a kind." I wanted to beat Iggy to the punch. When he said it, it came off as somewhat arrogant.

"Glinda, tell Diego and Camila what you need."

I pulled out a chair and sat down. "I need to find a spell that will wow the average human into thinking I can read their minds."

Levy sat next to me. "What Glinda is saying is that the spell doesn't actually have to work. She'll have two people with her who will let her know who is telling the truth. She just needs the possible thieves to believe she can do it."

Camila's brows scrunched. "I'm confused. Why have a spell at all if you have two mind readers with you?"

That was easy to answer. "Mind readers are great if the person you're reading doesn't try to block you. Both my cousin and my friend Penny have been wrong in the past, because the person was able to close off his mind. I thought the spell might distract the suspects enough to keep their minds open." Or the spell would make them block everyone in the room, but that was the chance I had to take.

Diego smiled. "Gotcha. You need something like a puff of smoke or a real magic trick, like the type that is performed on stage."

"That won't work," Iggy said.

Really? What did he know about magic shows? I'd never taken him to one. "Why is that?"

"It will look fake."

"Being fancy makes it look fake? What are you suggesting? That I change an iguana into a rabbit? That would be pretty spectacular."

"That would be a real travesty!" Iggy dipped his head and squinted at me. Clearly, he was not amused by my attempt at humor.

Levy held up a finger. "I've seen petals float in the air and then disappear."

"Wow. Really?"

He nodded. "I haven't done it myself, but how about if

we take a look for some spells that are spectacular, and if we get lucky, it can detect if a person is lying at the same time."

I smiled. "That would be too good to be true. Wouldn't it be cool if there is a spell that can make their eyes change colors if they lie?"

Camila whistled. "If we find that one, I'll learn the spell."

The group laughed. Levy, Camila, and Diego searched the library shelves for books they thought might be useful. From the large pile they were collecting, this could take days to go through them all. And that was time we didn't have.

When the three of them thought they had enough reference material, we all grabbed a book or two and began our search. My first one had a table of contents, but I wasn't sure if I should search for a mind-reading spell or one that had some spectacular visual effects.

It was about an hour into our search when Diego leaned back. "I have something."

"What is it?" I asked.

"It involves flower petals lifting up slightly and then fluttering—though not disappearing—in the air. But wait, there is more. It claims that everyone in the room will be so mesmerized by this effect, the spell will make every person tell the truth—at least those who are watching."

"I better tell the sheriff to keep his eyes closed, though I don't think he lies about anything."

"I'll close mine, too," Iggy announced.

"Are you saying you lie a lot?" Now he was being silly.

"No, but I might spill the beans and say you've never done this kind of spell before."

That would be something he'd do. "Definitely keep your

eyes closed then." I turned to Diego. "That sounds amazing. There has to be a catch."

"Yeah, there is. The ingredients should be easy to get a hold of, but the spell requires quite a lot of witch power."

I slumped in my seat. "Which I don't have, unless Rihanna and Penny can join forces with me."

"It doesn't mention anything about being able to join powers, but you've performed some pretty complicated spells in the past, and if I recall, they have worked."

I had been able to cloak myself, and I had erected an invisible barrier that caught some thieves. "True, but my abilities are inconsistent."

"Try it. No matter the level of witch, I bet all of them had to practice to get the petals to rise and flutter. As for getting people to tell the truth? You might have to rely on your friends."

That worked for me. "Let's say the spell succeeds. Does it specify how long after I perform the spell that I should ask these people if they stole Alex's necklace? Should I ask them one at a time? And if so, will the spell last that long?"

Diego ran a finger down the page. "It's not specific. Maybe ask the person who stole the necklace to raise his or her hand. That would shorten the questioning time frame."

That was ingenious. "I can try that."

"There's one other thing," he said.

Of course there was. "What is that?"

"The lifting of the petals isn't just a distraction. It's necessary for the truth telling part of the spell to work."

"Then I'll have to try to get the petals to rise, but if I can't, I'll have to rely on my friends to let me know who is telling the truth."

Diego smiled. "Whatever happens, I'm betting their reaction to your attempt at magic will be enough to distract them long enough for your friends to delve into their minds."

Rihanna might be able to do that but not Penny. "I hope so." I turned to Levy. "I can't thank you enough for helping me once again."

"Aw shucks. It was nothing. You know I always like to help."

Before Iggy and I took off, Camila made a copy of the spell. "Good luck."

"Thanks."

The list of ingredients looked fairly standard. My next stop needed to be the Hex and Bones store to gather what was required for the spell. Once I pulled out of the parking lot, Iggy poked his head out of my bag. "You do remember that both Hugo and Genevieve can move objects with their minds, right? You don't even need to do the spell correctly."

"I know, but I want to do this."

"Oo-kay," Iggy said, sounding quite disappointed.

"Maybe we can ask Hugo to come to the session and help in a different way." I would have to tell Andorra that he wasn't to do anything to help with the spell unless it was absolutely necessary.

"Yippee!"

On the way back, I called Jaxson who answered right away. "Any luck?"

"Yes. I'm driving back now. Can you and Rihanna meet us at Hex and Bones? I'll be needing her for my plan to work."

"Sure. See you in a few."

I didn't want to bother Penny and ask her to join us just so that she could watch me practice. Even though she didn't practice witchcraft herself very often, I had faith that she'd get it right on the first try. I asked Rihanna to be there, because I wanted her input in case things didn't go as planned.

As soon as we arrived back to Witch's Cove, I parked in front of our office and then walked across the street to the store. I didn't want to tell Alex yet what I'd planned in case I couldn't get the spell to work.

Inside, when I spotted Bertha, Elizabeth, and Andorra, I waved to each of them. Since I wanted all three to know what was going on, I motioned them to the counter. No one was in the store at the time, so I didn't feel guilty taking them away from any customers.

"What's up?" Andorra asked.

I outlined my plan and then placed the list of ingredients on the counter. "Do you have all of these, Bertha?"

"Let me see." She adjusted her glasses and read the list. "I sure do. I'll grab everything you need. Well, except for the petals."

Iggy poked his head out of my bag. "I'll donate some hibiscus flowers for the cause."

I smiled. "I think they might be a bit too big. I was thinking more like rose petals."

"Why not try Oglethorpes Flower Shop?" Elizabeth said. "They have them this time of year."

"Perfect." I pulled out my phone to see if maybe Jaxson and Rihanna could pick up a couple of flowers on their way here. As soon as the phone rang, it sounded as if Jaxson's cell was already inside the store. I looked up, and there they were.

Both of them came over. Jaxson leaned over and kissed me on the cheek. "What's up?"

"Could you pick up two or three roses for me? It's for the spell."

"Sure. You need Rihanna here, right?"

"I do."

Jaxson smiled. "Be right back."

With the ingredients being collected, I needed to talk with Hugo and maybe Genevieve. "Are our two special people in back?"

Bertha smiled. "They are." She nodded to her granddaughters. "You two should go. Glinda might need your expertise."

"I most certainly will," I said.

The four of us and Iggy went into the back room where Genevieve was facing Hugo, waving her hands in the air but saying nothing. Ah, telepathy at its best. What she was communicating to him was anyone's guess, but the moment Iggy popped his head out of my purse, Hugo smiled. Wow. I didn't get to see that reaction often—if ever.

When I neared, Iggy practically launched himself into Hugo's arms. "He likes you, Hugo."

The gargoyle nodded and cradled Iggy.

"Did you find out who stole the real necklace?" Genevieve asked.

"No, which is why I'm here. I'm hoping both of you can help."

"Oh, thank goodness," Hugo's better half said. "It was getting pretty boring around here."

I doubted that. "Let's take a seat, and I'll explain my

plan." We all sat down. "Once I've practiced and can do the spell that I'll tell you about in a moment, I'll ask Steve to call in the potential thieves to the station." I explained why I thought it was an inside job.

"I agree," Andorra said. "Someone planned to make the swap when Mrs. Coronado was out and about on her vacation. Why else make a duplicate?"

"Exactly. It's possible this person hoped to use it only a few times and then return the original." I explained that Rihanna and Penny would be there to let me know if anyone was lying.

"Glinda?" Rihanna said. I nodded. "Don't you think the suspects will think it a little odd if Penny and I are in the room to listen to them? I mean, one of us could pretend to be some kind of court reporter, but we'd need a machine for that."

I smiled. "That is where either Hugo, Genevieve, or both come in. They will cloak themselves and hold onto you as they teleport into the sheriff's conference room. They—and you—will remain cloaked during the proceedings." I looked over at the two gargoyles. "That is doable, right?"

Genevieve waved a dismissive hand. "No problem."

I swear the woman picked up human actions quicker than anyone. "That's great."

"Then what?" Elizabeth asked.

"This will be the tricky part. My spell is designed to elevate rose petals out of a bowl, which I will attempt to do."

"I still think you should ask Hugo to help," Iggy said once again.

"He'll be busy keeping cloaked." Yes, I could have him do

it, but I had my pride. "Anyway, the spell, in theory, will force people to tell the truth. I know Hugo can do that, too, but there will be five people, which is why I want to use magic. Even if I fail, if these people believe it is a truth spell, someone might crack."

"If I'm invisible, how can I signal to you if the person is lying? It's not like I can speak without alerting everyone to my presence," Rihanna said.

"I can translate," Iggy said.

What was he talking about? "How?"

Iggy turned to Hugo, and I had to assume Iggy was checking with his friend to make sure his plan would work.

Just then, Jaxson came in, waved three roses, and then slipped in behind Rihanna and sat down.

"I got this. So listen." Iggy acted as if he was now running The Pink Iguana Sleuths. Sheesh.

"I'm listening."

"I'll be on your lap while you are doing the spell. Rihanna and Penny can relay to Hugo or Genevieve if the person is lying—using a kind of Morse Code signal. Then Hugo will tell me, and I'll tap your leg: One if the person is lying and two if the person is telling the truth."

Iggy had come up with a lot of plans over the years, but this one was one of his best yet. "We might have to upgrade your detective status." To what exactly, I didn't know.

"I can be Sergeant Iggy."

I wasn't sure a sergeant ranked above a detective, but I'd let him have the title if he wanted it.

Bertha came in. "I have all of the ingredients."

"I guess this means it's time to give this spell a dry run."

"You got this, pink lady," Jaxson said with a grin.

We'd soon find out. I moved over to a table that was near the front of the room and then set out the ingredients.

"Let me pull off the petals for you," Rihanna said.

"Thank you." While she did that, I read over the spell. It was in Old English, but that was okay since I would be reading it. I was just happy I didn't have to memorize it.

To be honest, I had no idea if this would work, but the suspects wouldn't know if it did or didn't.

It appeared as if Bertha had provided me with twice as much as what I needed. Most likely, one set was to practice with and the other to do the spell.

"I'm pretty good with spells," Elizabeth said. "Would you like me to do it instead?"

"I'd like to try first, but if I can't do it, I will absolutely ask you to do it." I didn't want my ego to get in the way of finding the thief.

I carefully mixed everything, and then placed the petals on top of the other ingredients. This spell required a Sterno can, that when lit, would aid in the levitation of the petals. Once they were in the air, I was to say the spell. The problem was that I didn't know how long I had before the petals fell. When they did, would the suspects think they were free to lie?

"If someone confesses," Andorra said, "how much jail time will they get? Or will they just return the necklace and pay a fine?"

"I have no idea. The punishment isn't the reason for the spell." Whoops. I might have let the cat out of the bag, so to speak. I looked around at those present. If I couldn't trust them, I couldn't trust anyone. "Okay, here's the real reason I need to find the necklace, but you can't tell anyone."

They looked at each other. Well, not Rihanna, Jaxson, or Iggy since they already knew.

"Yes?" Andorra asked.

"Alex is alive." As expected, everyone talked at once—everyone but Hugo, of course, since he couldn't talk.

I explained when and how I learned about it, as well as how Alex managed to survive. "Right now, she is staying in Rihanna's room at the office with her bodyguard. If someone finds out she is not dead, they might try again, so mums the word."

Naturally, everyone agreed.

"That means Hugo was right in claiming the necklace Gustavo had was a fake," Andorra said.

"He most certainly was."

She smiled. "Then let's fire up this puppy and get those rose petals floating!"

Chapter Sixteen

NOT LONG AFTER successfully completing the spell at the Hex and Bones, I called Steve to let him know we were ready. Soon afterward, Jaxson, Iggy, and I entered the sheriff's office where I immediately checked out the glass enclosed conference room. I found it empty of the suspects. Good. Jaxson needed time to get settled in Steve's office, and I needed some time to set up my bowl and spell ingredients. Besides, it wasn't time for them to be here.

"Iggy?"

He poked his head out of my purse. "Yes?"

"Let me know when Hugo and Genevieve arrive invisibly with Rhianna and Penny, okay?"

He looked over at the glass enclosure. "They're here already."

"Oh, okay, thanks." I'd forgotten I couldn't see an invisible person.

Steve came out of his office. "Jaxson, you'll be in my office with Nash. The cameras are running already, so you two will hear and see everything that goes on."

"Sounds good." Jaxson gave me a quick kiss. "Make them all confess."

"I'll try." Actually, all I wanted was for the petals to rise.

Then I would try to learn who had taken Alex's necklace.

With my gear in hand, Iggy and I headed into the conference room. As I walked toward one end of the room, I hit an invisible wall and nearly dropped the bowl.

"Hey, watch it." That was Rihanna.

"Sorry. I didn't know you were there."

"Only kidding. Where do you think we should stand?" she asked. "We don't want to get in the way."

In the past, Steve always had the suspects sit with their backs to the main office. "How about facing the glass wall? That way you can watch their faces. Penny is here, right?"

"I am. This is so exciting. I've never been invisible before."

"It's a change, for sure. The hard part will be to remember that they can't see you, which means you can't talk."

"I'll try to remember."

"All five of you know the signal for lying versus telling the truth, right?" I looked down at Iggy to make sure he understood he was included in this.

"Yes, Glinda," Genevieve said.

"Okay." I took my seat at one end and placed the ingredients in the bowl. I then set the written spell next to it. My only goal was to levitate the petals and make sure the suspects believed that the act would force them to tell the truth. I had no illusions of grandeur to think I had enough witch power to get them to confess.

Steve poked his head in. "They are on their way."

I inhaled. Show time. It wasn't as if I hadn't done spells before, and to be honest, this one wasn't even that important. Sure, Alex might grow old if no one confessed to having taken her necklace, but it wasn't as if she'd die without it—or at least I hope not.

One by one, the group filed in, and I studied each of them, hoping the word guilty would be written across their foreheads. Sadly, they all looked more concerned than scared. The only one whose appearance shocked me was Alex's husband. The poor man looked as if he hadn't slept since his wife's death. I hoped we could tell him sooner rather than later that Alex was alive.

"I don't understand why I'm here, Gustavo." Jodi had whispered her concern, but it was loud enough for me to hear.

I figured she'd be upset. After all, she hadn't been in town during the theft.

"The sheriff probably has news about Mom," Alex's son told her.

Yes, Steve did have news, but he wouldn't be sharing it any time soon.

Once Steve told everyone to take a seat, he sat down. "I'm sorry to have to call you in during these sad times, but I've asked Glinda to help find out who stole Mrs. Coronado's pink pearl necklace."

"Why?" Gustavo asked. "Mom is gone. She won't need it. Finding her killer is more important."

He was right about that.

"Several crimes were committed. I thought I'd start with the easier of the two. That might lead me to your mom's killer," Steve said.

"Right. Of course." Gustavo seemed to understand.

"Considering a fake necklace was made to resemble Mrs. Coronado's prized necklace, I feel it is reasonable to assume that someone in the family took the real one and had a replacement made before coming to Witch's Cove," Steve said.

"That's ridiculous," Alex's husband responded. "No one would do that."

Hmm. I thought he protested a bit too much.

"That may be, Mr. Coronado," Steve said. "This is why I've asked Glinda to conduct a spell that will compel everyone in the room to tell the truth about what they know in regards to the theft. Anyone who lies will suffer physical consequences."

They will? I never said anything like that. For a man who didn't lie, I was surprised he'd say that. Maybe he thought I wouldn't be able to convince them that I was serious otherwise. Whatever.

"May I begin?" I asked.

"Certainly."

I looked at each of the five people. "While I am doing the spell, please do not speak. If you do, it will make you look guilty."

I had no idea why I said that, but it sounded good. Since I already had everything ready to go, all I had to do was light the Sterno can. Once the ingredients heated, the petals should lift up and flutter, like they had at the Hex and Bones. "The rose petals will be able to sense truth versus deceit. Once they rise, I will ask you whether you had anything to do with taking the necklace. Please, don't lie. I'll know." Or Rihanna and Penny would.

When no one called me a fraud, I recited the spell. My hands were shaking, and my voice was thick with anxiety.

Once I finished, I expected the flowers to rise at least a little. However, nothing in the bowl moved. This was bad. I couldn't ask the suspects anything until the petals performed some magic. If I knew how to urge them to float, I would. It had worked before so what had I done differently this time? Saying the spell again might do the trick, but it would make me look incompetent.

Just as I was about to call it quits, the petals lifted into the air. Yes! I did it—or else Genevieve or Hugo had a hand in it. For now, I chose to remain in denial. I wanted, or rather needed, to believe I had been successful.

Instead of asking the group to raise a hand if they stole the necklace, I decided to do one person at a time. I started with the easiest person. "Jodi, did you have anything to do with the theft of the necklace or have any knowledge that someone was planning to steal it?"

Her eyes widened. "No. I wasn't even in town."

Iggy tapped my leg twice to indicate she was telling the truth. "Thank you. Dante Diaz, did you have anything to do with the theft of the necklace?"

"Absolutely not. I liked Alex very much. I never would have done that to her."

Once more Iggy tapped my leg twice. That meant that neither Jodi nor Dante had been involved in the theft, which didn't surprise me, as I figured they were innocent. I repeated the same question to Alex's assistant, Nina, and she, too, told the truth. That meant either Alex's son or husband had taken the necklace.

The words of Alex's mother came back to me. She'd said that if someone else wore the necklace that there would be consequences. Looking at Alex's husband, it seemed as if he might be the guilty party.

"I'm going to skip Gustavo for now."

"Why? You think I took Mom's necklace?"

Whoa. I struck a nerve there. "I didn't say anything."

"Then why skip me? You aren't going to pin this on me. It was Dad. He wanted to look young like Mom."

And there we had it. I didn't need Iggy to tap my leg to let me know that Gustavo was telling the truth.

"Mr. Coronado," Steve said. "What do you have to say for yourself?"

"I...ah...." He lowered his head. "I only meant to wear it at night. I honestly didn't think Alex would notice."

"And when she reported it stolen, why didn't you say anything then?" Steve asked.

"I planned to replace the copy with the real one in a few days. Just as I was about to put the other necklace in the safe for Alex to find, she woke up. I had to hide the fake one under the bed."

The man was a waste of skin. I wasn't sure what Steve was going to do now. Arrest him?

"Where is the real necklace?" Steve asked.

"Back at the hotel."

"I'll have Deputy Solano escort you there so you can retrieve it. We'll need it for evidence. Everyone stay here for a moment."

Steve stepped out of the room, even though Nash could hear every word of the conversation. This was my chance to ask Alex's husband if he was the one to cut her hose.

"Mr. Coronado, did you kill your wife?"

The man turned a dark shade of red. "No. Never. I loved Alex. It's why I wanted to look young. It was for *her* sake that I took the necklace."

I didn't need anyone to tell me part of what he said might have been true, but that the rest was a lie. He wanted to look younger for himself I bet. Alex never mentioned that she was embarrassed by having an older looking husband.

Steve and Nash returned. "Mr. Coronado, would you please go now with the Deputy?"

The son looked disgusted as the father nodded and followed Nash out. That or Gustavo was a good actor.

"Can we leave?" Gustavo said. "You have your thief."

While we had everyone here, I probably should ask them if they'd tried to kill Alex, but during my little demonstration, I had a better idea. I admit I probably shouldn't have questioned Alex's husband, but I was impatient. I wanted to know the identity of the killer immediately.

Steve looked over at me, and I nodded. "Yes, but stay in town," he said.

"For how long?" Gustavo asked. "With Mom dead, we have a lot of work to do. We can't remain here indefinitely. We have a company to run. Without her, there will have to be a lot of changes."

Did these changes involve him running the company?

"I imagine we'll get to the bottom of this in the next few days," Steve said.

I hoped that was true.

Once everyone left, Hugo and Genevieve uncloaked themselves, along with Rihanna and Penny.

"That was so cool and strange at the same time," Penny

said.

"Tell me about it," I said. "Thank goodness, Hugo could communicate with Iggy, who could tap my leg. What do you all think of Mr. Coronado's confession?"

"He was so stressed out, that there were times when he blocked his thoughts," Rihanna said. "We were lucky that he confessed."

"I agree. Any thoughts on who might have cut Alex's hose?"

All four shook their heads. "Have a seat for a moment. I have another idea." I looked up at the camera. "Jaxson, if you can hear us, can you come in here?" A moment later, Jaxson entered.

"You said you have another idea?" Steve asked. "I have to say I was skeptical that the first one would work, but I guess it did."

"I do have a plan, but it's a bit unorthodox."

Jaxson smiled. "When are your ideas anything but unorthodox?"

"You're funny, but you're right this time. I thought we could do a séance and have Alex's voice piped into the room here. Naturally, she'd be in Steve's office and could see those present, but if she accuses someone of the crime we could watch their reaction."

Steve dipped his head. "Did Alex suddenly remember who cut her hose?"

"No, but if she points a finger at say, her son, then if the dad is guilty, he'll confess so that Gustavo won't go to jail for the rest of his life. And I bet his wife would admit to the murder to protect Gustavo if she had tried to kill Alex. Or am

I being naive?"

"Most definitely naive, but Jodi wasn't on the boat, remember?" Steve said.

"Dave said she could have arrived at the area before he did and waited in the cave."

"Ah, yes. He did say that. Your new plan seems to depend on Alex being a good actress. If no one confesses, I don't know how we'll prove anything."

That was the sad part. "I know."

Steve looked around. "Do either of you two shifters have any better ideas?"

Genevieve looked over at Hugo and then turned back to Steve. "Nothing that would hold up in court. I mean, Hugo might be able to extract the information out of each person, but there are two issues with that. One is that it would be his word—or maybe mine—against the hose cutter's. And secondly, not all people are susceptible to Hugo's prying. We got lucky the last time with the person who killed Drake's friend, but she was a witch, so that had made it easier."

"Then I guess we go with Glinda's proposal. When can you be ready?" Steve asked me.

"I'll have to confer with Alex, naturally. Then we'll have to come up with some questions that I can ask to make sure I lead the discussion in the right direction. But that shouldn't take long. I'd say tomorrow sometime."

"Darn. I work tomorrow," Penny said.

I hadn't thought of asking Rihanna and Penny to return, but there was no reason for them not to be there. I looked over at Genevieve. "Would it be possible to do this cloaking thing again?"

"No problem. Anything to solve a crime."

I smiled. "Thank you both."

"Glinda, shall I set up the interview for three thirty to allow Penny to get off work and come over?"

"Perfect." I turned to her. "You can change out of your noisy penny skirt at my apartment."

"You got it."

I pushed back my chair and turned to Jaxson. "Ready to see if we can pull this off?"

"You bet."

Just as we were leaving, Nash returned, holding up the necklace. Alex would be so happy to have it back. I rushed up to him. "I guess this means the husband really was the thief."

"Apparently, but the man is a mess. I don't think he killed his wife—or rather tried to kill her."

"Interesting. While I deliver this to its rightful owner, how about Steve tells you about my new plan?"

He smiled. "Another Glinda special?"

At least he didn't make it sound like a bad thing. "I hope so."

With the necklace in hand—well, it was actually in my purse—we headed out.

"Rihanna and Penny, can you two come to the shop tomorrow before we have the séance?" Genevieve asked. "We'll leave from there."

"Works for me," my cousin said, and Penny nodded.

Chapter Seventeen

"DO YOU THINK Alex will be okay with attempting a fake séance?" I asked Jaxson, Rihanna, and Penny as we crossed the street back to our office.

"Why wouldn't she be? She needs to know who tried to kill her," he said.

"I know, but she'll have to point a finger at someone she cares about."

Jaxson placed a hand on my back as I stepped up on the curb. "I'm sure you'll suggest someone, and then Alex will say she was just following your instructions."

He was smart. "I guess so. I just worry that no one will confess."

"Negative thinking won't get you anywhere."

"I need to remember that."

Once we reached Penny's car, I hugged her goodbye and thanked her again for helping.

"I loved it. I appreciate you asking me."

"Of course."

Just as we made it to the stairs, two seagulls flew close overhead and squawked loudly, causing Iggy to poke his head out of my bag. "See? They know where I am at all times."

"I thought you wanted the seagulls to be here so they

could keep the rats away?"

"I do, but I don't. I mean, I don't want Tippy anywhere near me."

I had too much on my mind to deal with Iggy's angst, so I didn't engage in further conversation with him. Instead, I headed upstairs. To prevent Alex from having to dive for cover when I jiggled the door handle, I said I'd tap on the door three times, wait a second, and then tap twice more. I did that combination now and then unlocked the door.

Mr. Ortega was in the main room. "Where's Alex?" I asked.

"In the bedroom."

I withdrew the necklace from my purse. "Ta-da."

His eyes widened. "You have it. She'll be so happy. I'll let her know."

A second after her bodyguard knocked on the bedroom door, Alex came rushing out. "You have it?"

I held it out. "It was a group effort."

She took it from me and then hugged me, Rihanna, and Jaxson in turn. "Thank you, thank you." She clasped it around her neck. "I only kind of want to know, but who was the thief?"

"Your husband."

Her brows pinched. "Ricardo? Why?"

I explained that he thought she didn't want to be with an older man. "I have to tell you, if he wore that necklace for any length of time, it didn't work. On the contrary, it made him look worse."

She walked over to the sofa and sat down, acting as if the weight of the information was too much. "That's what Mom said would happen, or rather what her ghost said would happen."

Her mom said there would be consequences, but she never specifically said what they would be. Aging fast would be a bad one, though. "Yes."

"So, Ricardo just confessed?"

"Not at first." I went through everything that happened. "I can't say why I skipped over Gustavo. I must have had a sense that your husband was guilty."

She shook her head. "What will happen to him?"

"I don't know. You and he are married, so the courts might think that the necklace is kind of his property. I really can't say since I'm not a lawyer."

"It might depend on whether you want to press charges," Rihanna tossed in.

How did she know that? Oh, that's right. My cousin had mentioned she was taking a class in criminal justice at school.

"It doesn't matter." Alex said. "I won't press charges, but I also won't be staying with a man who would do something like that to me. He knew how upset I was, yet he kept the truth from me."

I wouldn't stay with him either.

Jaxson stepped toward the kitchen. "Drinks anyone?"

We all asked for something, including Alex's bodyguard. As soon as Jaxson fixed the drinks and then returned, Iggy must have decided he was tired of being in my purse, or else he'd fallen asleep, since he crawled out. I swear he could nod off anywhere.

"I have a plan for how to find your attempted killer," I said.

Alex and Mr. Ortega perked up. "How? Admitting to borrowing a necklace is one thing, but saying he or she wanted me dead is another."

Is that what her husband did? He borrowed her necklace? If so, why have a duplicate made? I probably would never learn the real reason for that one, nor did it really matter.

"I know, which is why I have a plan that involves a séance."

"With my Mom?"

"Not exactly. With you."

Alex looked at Mr. Ortega and then back at me. "Correct me if I'm wrong, but I thought the person needed to be dead in order to do a séance."

"They do. That's why ours will be a fake one."

Alex sat up straighter. "Thank goodness for that."

I appreciated her good attitude. "Conducting a séance with a living person I can pull off, but the tricky part will be getting the ghost of Alex Coronado to force someone to confess."

"I don't know how to do that, but we have all night to figure it out!"

ONCE MORE, JAXSON spent the night at his place to make sure Rihanna remained safe, while Iggy promised to protect me. In all honesty, few would dare to break into my apartment above the restaurant, especially with all the conspicuous cameras around. Not only that, we were situated across the street from the sheriff's department. Having my apartment on the second floor helped, too. The stairs creaked, which meant Iggy would hear any intruder.

Despite believing I wasn't in danger, I couldn't sleep. What had I been thinking that a fake séance would work? Sure, I had faith that Alex's voice would transmit nicely over the microphone, but if anyone spotted the device, they'd know it was all for show. Or would they? They'd recognize her voice, and since no one knew that Alex was alive, they would have to believe she was talking to them from the beyond. Right?

For the next few hours, I tossed and turned until a thin stream of light filtered in past my curtained windows. After another hour, I gave up on getting any more rest and slipped out of bed. First order of business was to take a shower.

Having warm water pour over my body could do amazing things to release my mind from troubling thoughts. And where did that brain of mine wander? To our go-to gargoyle shifters, of course. I wondered if maybe Hugo or Genevieve could put on a different kind of show for us. I know that both could cloak themselves, but were they able to partially cloak themselves and appear transparent? In other words, could Genevieve make herself look like the ghost of Alex Coronado? That would convince everyone that Alex was really dead.

I turned off the water, stepped out of the shower, and dried off. It was then that I envisioned Hugo, in his stealth form, sneaking around each person and touching them to make them believe that spirits were everywhere.

Shivers raced down my spine at that creepy thought. The plan sounded good in theory, but there were issues. If Genevieve and Hugo were busy scaring people, how could

Penny and Rihanna be in the room without drawing attention?

I snapped my fingers. Yes. I got it. I'd tell the suspects that I needed several witches to help me with the séance. And that was the truth. I don't think Jaxson would mind staying with Nash in Steve's office to watch what was going on instead of participating.

With renewed energy, I dressed, gathered my iguana, and headed over to the Hex and Bones. Before I raised Alex's hopes, I wanted to see if our resident gargoyles could pull this off.

"Do you think they can do this?" I asked Iggy once I divulged my plan.

"Hugo can do anything."

Why did I think he'd give me a serious answer? We crossed the street and entered the Hex and Bones. Since they'd just opened, Elizabeth was off to the side placing candles on a shelf, Andorra was adding some t-shirts to the rack, and Bertha was at the cash register counting the money.

Bertha looked up and smiled. "Glinda! You're up early."

"Tell me about it. I'm up because I need to discuss a few things with Genevieve and Hugo."

"They're in the back."

Andorra waved and came over. "I heard you and the gang were successful in retrieving the necklace yesterday."

"We were thanks to everyone's help. Needless to say, Alex is a very happy camper."

"I can imagine. So now what?"

"I have a plan. Want to join me in the back?"

"Absolutely," Andorra said.

Once in the back room, I handed Iggy over to Hugo since the big guy liked to hold my familiar.

"I think I know how we can figure out who killed Alex," I said.

"This sounds like fun," Genevieve said.

"Let's take a seat. I think better sitting down." I began by describing how Alex would be in the sheriff's office, answering the séance questions we would prepare in advance. "The sound will be piped into the glass enclosed room. Naturally, all present will believe Alex is a ghost since they all think she is dead."

Andorra smiled. "That sounds great. Can I help?"

"Yes. I'd like you to be there to give credence to the séance. Rihanna and Penny will also be there. I just need to tell them it won't involve being invisible this time."

"And us?" Genevieve asked.

I winced a bit. "I fear that when the suspects hear Alex's voice, they might be looking for some kind of device that is transmitting the sound. Naturally, there will be one. But what if you could sort of, kind of become translucent? I'm not suggesting you wear a sheet in order to look like a ghost, but could you maybe be halfway between visible and invisible? You could even flicker on and off if you want." Assuming she could. "Are you able to do that?"

Genevieve smiled. "You mean like this?"

One second she was standing there, and the next she was barely there. A real ghost was a bit more opaque, but she'd do. We didn't want anyone to see her face and say it wasn't Alex—which it wouldn't be—so the more transparent the better.

My pulse skyrocketed in excitement. "Yes, that's perfect!"

"I think Genevieve should wear some of Alex's clothes, just in case she turns more opaque," Andorra said.

"I like that idea. Procuring the clothes would require a bit of stealth, but I'm sure we can figure something out—with the help from our sheriff's department, of course."

Genevieve turned solid again and then looked over at Hugo. "I realize that Hugo doesn't look like Alex, but can he help in some way, too?"

"Yes. I thought Hugo could cloak himself and then scare the suspects a bit by tapping on their shoulder or maybe sending a wave of cold air over them. I'm betting they've all read about how one can tell if a ghost is close by."

"How?" Genevieve asked.

I was surprised she didn't know, but then why should she? "When you are kissed by a blast of cool air, it means a ghost or some supernatural being is near."

Hugo's hands instantly became blocks of ice. While he'd done this before, I'd not been there for the demonstration. He cloaked himself, and a moment later, a wave of cold air skipped across my face, causing chills to literally run up and down my arms.

"That is perfect. You two are amazing."

"I told you they were," Iggy chimed in.

No, he said Hugo could do anything, but I wasn't going to argue semantics.

As for Iggy, I needed to find something for him to do. He could cloak himself, but his ability to stay cloaked for a long time was questionable. By this afternoon, I would figure something out.

"Can you two be ready around three? I'll drop off something of Alex's that Genevieve can wear. Steve can ask our guests to arrive around three thirty. Sound good?"

"Yes, I'm really excited," Andorra said.

"So am I." In part because my magic skills were not really required to pull this off. It would be up to our gargoyles and Alex to be convincing. I certainly wouldn't be upset if by some chance Hugo did his mind bending on a few of the suspects. I'd never know, and he wouldn't appear on camera.

"Iggy, do you want to stay here and come over with Hugo at three?"

"Yes! I'll come over with Hugo."

I figured he'd say that.

I waved goodbye to Bertha and Elizabeth as I headed out. On the way to the sheriff's office, I called Jaxson.

"Where are you?" he asked.

"I need to ask Steve to take care of something, and then I thought maybe we could grab a bite to eat. I'm starving."

"I'm over at the office, and Mr. Ortega was discussing that very fact. How about he and I pick up enough for all of us. We can eat back here."

"Sounds perfect. See you in a few."

The fastest breakfast place might be the Tiki Hut Grill since Aunt Fern would make sure they had their food prepared quickly.

I stepped into the sheriff's department, and there was Pearl manning her station. "Glinda. Any news?"

News? About what? Who in theory had killed Alex? "No, but I have a plan."

She smiled. "You always have a plan. Nash and Steve are in his office. Go on back."

"Thanks."

Chapter Eighteen

I LIGHTLY TAPPED on the sheriff's door and then pushed it open.

Steve looked up. "Come in."

Nash moved his chair over, and I sat in the one next to him. "I need a small favor to help solve the case of who attempted to kill Alex."

"What kind of favor?"

I explained how I'd like Genevieve to be ghost-like and pretend to be Alex. "It will add a lot of credibility to my plan. But that requires you to go into Alex's room and grab something of hers for Genevieve to wear."

"Why not ask her to do it?" he asked.

"I could, but who knows what she'd choose. I trust you more."

Steve leaned back in his chair. "No problem, but I'll have to figure out a way to get in without arousing suspicion from Mr. Coronado."

"You could ask the maid to do it. Or ask the front desk to let you know when he goes out to eat or something."

He nodded. "Nash and I will think of something. Is the plan set then?"

"I hope so." I went over it one more time. "I think being

touched by an invisible, icy cold entity would convince even the biggest skeptic that ghosts are real."

"It would me," Nash said.

"How long do you need to get the outfit and then set up the room?" I asked. We had tentatively set the time for three thirty.

Steve checked his watch. "How about I contact you once I deliver the outfit to Genevieve?"

I smiled. "Such service!"

"We aim to please."

I smiled. With that chore complete, I headed back to the office, ready to chow down. I hoped Alex would like the addition of a real apparition to the mix.

The moment I entered, the rich aroma of coffee, the sweet scent of sugary donuts, and the tangy smell of eggs filled the air. "This looks divine. Thank you."

Jaxson had set out the food on our small coffee table.

"Have a seat and dig in," he said.

He didn't have to ask twice. Everyone had already filled their plates and apparently were waiting for me before they started eating. I wanted to get the ball rolling on this new scheme of mine. "I had another thought about the séance."

"What's that?" Alex asked.

I told them about Genevieve's ability to appear translucent. "Since she's a bit more see-through than a real ghost, you can't see her face, but she might flicker and expose herself."

"How about if she wears one of my oversized beach hats? It might shield her face from view," Alex offered.

"Actually, I suggested to Steve that he pick up something of yours, but I'll text him to add the hat." I probably should have asked her first.

"Perfect."

"Glinda, you've never mentioned before what any ghost had worn during a séance," Jaxson said.

I had to think about that. "I'm not sure I paid attention. Before we were together, do you remember Morgan Oliver?"

"He was the dead guy who was shot in the back."

"Exactly. I remember his T-shirt had a red-stained hole in it. He was close to being opaque, but other ghosts are barely visible. Whatever transparency level Genevieve chooses will be okay. If she's dressed in one of Alex's outfits, no one will question it, as long as she keeps her head down."

"That sounds wonderful, except that I'm a witch," Alex said, "and I've never seen a ghost. Will these people be surprised when they see one?"

I hadn't thought of that. "Maybe, but it is a séance, and they'll think ghosts come to those. They won't know only a few can even see them."

She smiled. "I can tell you've thought this through."

"Not all the way through. Unexpected stuff happens all the time."

"Your sheriff will tell them everything will be recorded, right?" Alex asked.

"Yes. He kind of has to, even though it will probably keep them from confessing. Hopefully, they will be sufficiently scared and blurt something out.

Last night we'd come up with some sample questions, but if a ghost was floating around, and another was sending cold air across their bodies, I might only have their attention for a minute or two.

"What do you need from me?" she asked.

"You have the questions—as do I. We just have to decide where to begin. Are you okay with stating that your son cut your hose?"

She nodded. "He doesn't have the guts to do it, so I know he's innocent."

I hope she wasn't blinded by her love for Gustavo. "Nash didn't think your husband did it, so it doesn't leave us with many viable candidates."

"Ricardo could have hired someone to go down and cut my hose. It's something he'd do," she said.

That would put a crimp in things.

"Would you like me to be there?" Mr. Ortega asked.

"You could be, but why would you want to?"

"I don't mind saying that Alex felt threatened back in Atlanta, and that she suspected someone close to her wanted her dead. In fact, I'll say she suspected Gustavo was the one who wanted her out of the way—or any other person you wish me to accuse."

"I really appreciate it, but it might have more impact if I say it," Alex claimed.

"I'll do whatever you wish."

Jaxson finished off his coffee. "Glinda, how about if Mr. Ortega goes into the inquisition, for lack of a better word, and have Steve interview him. That might put the killer ill at ease. Geraldo can leave, and you can begin the séance."

I grabbed a donut and smiled. "I think that is brilliant. I knew there was a reason why I agreed to marry you."

"I hope that's not the only reason." He winked.

Heat raced up my face at the implication, forcing me to

clear my throat. "By the way, where is my cousin?" I asked, needing to change the subject.

"I drove her back here this morning to pick up her car. Rihanna wanted to give Alex some space," Jaxson said.

"I'll give her a call and let her know when to meet us."

ABOUT TWO HOURS later, I received the call from Steve that he had been able to get into Alex's room to borrow a thing or two for Genevieve, including a big, floppy beach hat.

"Did you give the items to Genevieve?"

"I did. What else do you need from me? The microphone and speaker have always been in the room, so all I need to do is turn on the system."

I didn't know that our conversations might have been recorded in the past. With nothing to hide, I had no problem with it. "I need a table with four chairs. I'll bring the candles."

"Can't you use the conference room table?"

"No, we have to touch hands, and I've tried it once before. It didn't work."

"Gotcha. See you around three or so?"

"We'll be there."

I called Penny and asked her to join all of us at our office instead of my apartment so we could rehearse what was going to happen once more. She could change there.

Penny must have run into Rihanna outside, because they arrived together at two thirty.

Penny's hair was pulled back into a neat bun, and her tailored navy-blue skirt and white blouse looked like she was dressed more for a court appearance than a séance, but far be it for me to say anything about how someone dressed.

"You dressed already," I said.

"Yeah, Fern let me change at her place."

"Cool." I motioned they have a seat.

Penny and Rihanna joined me on the sofa. Jaxson had borrowed a few chairs from Drake so everyone could sit.

"Steve has agreed to have Mr. Ortega go first," I said. "He will tell us how threatened Alex felt, and that she had a very good idea who was targeting her." I turned to Jaxson. "You still haven't learned who sent the emails, have you?"

"I was only able to trace them to the Atlanta area, but that's all. Sorry."

"No worries. I hope we won't need it. Should we invite Andorra and the gang over here?" And I missed Iggy.

"I think our gargoyles know what to do. As for Andorra, she just needs to sit at a table," Jaxson said.

He was right. Clearly, I was having some sort of anxiety over this. I turned to Alex. "Do you have any questions?"

"Yes. How should I sound? Do I try to make it seem as if I'm far away, or can I come on strong and accusatory?"

I knew which one she wanted. "To be honest, most ghosts sound as if it requires work to talk. Maybe that's why they don't stay around for long. When you think you've made your point, say you have to go. That way Genevieve will know it's time to disappear. We don't need her doing anything crazy."

Alex laughed. "That would be bad."

I discussed the logistics once more until it was time to leave. "Let's go find out who wants Alex dead."

"Is it safe to go outside? Someone may see me."

She had a point.

Rihanna stood. "Come with me. I'll make sure no one knows it's you."

My cousin had dressed me before, and she was good with disguises. Her eye for style was excellent too. "Hurry though."

"You guys go, and Penny and I will escort Alex over. It will look less conspicuous that way."

"You're right."

Mr. Ortega, Jaxson, and I headed out. I assumed that Iggy would show up with Hugo at some point.

When we entered the sheriff's office, Pearl told us to go into the conference room where Steve and Nash were setting up the table. He glanced up and waved us in.

Once we entered the room, they were moving the big table slightly out of the way to give the card table more room.

"Does this work?" Steve asked.

"It's perfect. Rihanna and Penny are fixing up Alex in some disguise and will be over soon."

"Perfect. We have twenty minutes before Nash brings the five of them over." Steve turned to Mr. Ortega and Jaxson. "Gentlemen, if you would come with me."

"Good luck," Jaxson said.

"Thanks."

As soon as they left, the room seemed eerily quiet. I couldn't recall if I'd been in here alone before. That shouldn't matter. I had work to do. I placed my candles on the table, along with matches, and then arranged the chairs.

A few minutes later, Rihanna and Penny arrived but without Alex. Rihanna smiled as they both entered the conference room.

"Where is our guest of honor?" I asked.

"I thought it would be better if Genevieve delivered her in person."

That was very clever. "I assume our lady gargoyle will teleport her directly into Steve's office?"

"She will. And yes, Alex gave the okay for Genevieve's attire, with a few tweaks, of course."

"And where are Andorra, Hugo, and Iggy?"

Before she could answer, the front door opened, and Andorra came in carrying my iguana. I waved her in.

Andorra handed me Iggy. "This is so exciting. Where do you need me to sit?"

"I thought you and I would have the two worst seats since I'd like Rihanna and Penny to be able to see everyone's faces. It will be easier for them to tell if they are lying."

"Do you want me to kick you under the table if they aren't telling the truth?" Rihanna asked.

I hadn't thought of that. "We're sitting close. How about if you hold Iggy. If you tap his head once for a lie and twice for the truth, he can flick his tail and hit my leg the same number of times." I looked down at him. "How does that sound? It's an important role."

"I can do it."

I figured he'd like it. Steve knocked lightly on the door and came in. "I hope you are ready since Nash went to retrieve them."

"We are." He left, and I motioned we all take a seat. "Is Hugo with Genevieve?" I asked Andorra.

"Hugo is here, but he needs to remain cloaked."

"Oh. Hi, Hugo. Thanks again for helping." I felt dumb talking to the air, but it wasn't as if I had a choice.

"What's going to happen?" Andorra asked.

"Steve will ask Mr. Ortega a few questions, and then it will be our turn to start the séance." I had placed my questions on the table. "Fingers crossed this works."

It seemed like forever before the five suspects came in. I felt sorry for the truly innocent ones. It must be hard to trust that their lives were dependent on some mumbo-jumbo—or whatever they believed this to be.

Which of these people, if any, had wanted to harm Alex? And why? Was their hate so strong that they would risk spending the rest of their life in jail just to get rid of her? I guess so.

Nina, Alex's assistant, had said that the company lawyer was pretty cut throat. While he might have been capable of doing harm, I didn't see any good motive on his part. Nina would be out of a job she loved once Alex died, so she seemed innocent, too. As for Jodi, Gustavo's wife, I knew little about her. Could she have wanted her husband to have the chance to do more in the company? From what Nina said, he wasn't the most ambitious person, but that could be because his mom didn't really approve of him.

And Ricardo Coronado? He didn't appear to have even shaved today. What was up with that?

Before I could continue my analysis, Steve came in with Mr. Ortega. I had no idea if Genevieve was here yet, but if she wasn't, I figured Andorra might say something to delay the séance.

Steve motioned for the bodyguard to take a seat. "I'm sure you all know Geraldo Ortega, Alex's bodyguard. I've asked him to give his take on what happened in the few weeks prior to Alex's death." Steve nodded to him. "You can begin when you are ready."

Chapter Nineteen

I WATCHED THE group as Mr. Ortega listed the threatening emails. I could be wrong, but it didn't seem as if Mr. Coronado had any idea that this was going on. Nina and Dante, on the other hand, exchanged a few knowing glances.

Uh-oh. Had this murder attempt been a result of more than one person? I might believe it, if I could come up with a good motive.

I thought Steve would ask questions about the accusations in the emails, but he didn't. When Mr. Ortega finished delivering his information, Steve excused Alex's bodyguard. Since everything said was being piped into Steve's office, Genevieve would know she was up.

Steve told the group that he would be recording the session.

Gustavo huffed. "I don't believe in ghosts, but even if one showed up, you can't record them."

"Have you tried?" I asked. Yes, I know, this was Steve's show, but he was out of his element here.

"No."

"Okay then." I turned back to my fellow witches. "Ready, ladies?"

All of them nodded. I lit the candles, and then we

touched our finger tips. Since this was a fake séance, I had told them to keep their eyes open since they needed to be able to watch the people's reactions.

When they indicated they were ready, I began. "Alexandria Coronado. We are here today to assess who was responsible for your death. Can you tell us who cut your air hose?"

I knew she wasn't aware of the guilty party, but she could point a finger. I just hoped that my two gargoyle friends were ready to take over.

"Hello?" came a faint voice from the corner.

Whoa. That was Alex, and she sounded pretty ghost-like. I didn't see Genevieve yet, and I could only hope that if the three had come up with a different plan, it was better than the one I'd outlined.

I didn't want to check out the suspects as that would look a little contrived, but my two mind readers sure were observing them. I wish I could telepath with Rihanna right now to find out what everyone was thinking.

"Did anyone feel that?" Jodi said.

"Feel what?" Gustavo answered.

"A chill."

Hello, Hugo!

"Yes. Does that mean Mom is really here? How is that possible? Ghosts aren't real."

I'm glad Gustavo recognized that the chill meant the presence of a ghost. I had to intervene before things imploded. "Why can't they be real? When a person passes over, they can take on a sort of translucent form. No, they won't be wearing a sheet like in the movies, but you will be able to see her if she chooses to take that form. Sometimes ghosts merely speak through a person, however."

Just then, Genevieve fluttered in the corner. *You go, girl.* I didn't know she could come and go like that.

"What was that?" Mr. Coronado asked.

I looked over at the corner, acting as if I didn't know. "Mrs. Coronado? Is that you?"

"Yes. I don't have much time. I want him to pay."

"Him?" There were several males in the room.

"My son. He's been angry ever since I asked Ricardo to run the company with me."

Gustavo shoved back his chair. "She's lying. I loved my mother. I never would have killed her."

A second later he sat down, but it appeared as if Hugo was controlling him. "I was with my father the whole time we were down below. Ask him."

I kind of doubted the word of a thief would hold up in court.

Jodi shivered. "Can you turn down the air conditioner? It's freezing."

I needed to answer her. "It's Alex's ghost that is doing that."

"How can she be in two places at once?" Jodi questioned. "Never mind. Alex does what she wants to do. She always needed to control everything. My husband is fully capable of running the entire company, and yet she won't let him do anything." The bitterness that laced her tone almost dripped off her tongue.

"Jodi, that's not true," Gustavo said. "I don't want to spend every waking hour at the company. I want to be with you."

"I know, but now you can take over."

Gustavo stilled. "Jodi, what are you saying?"

Her mouth opened as if to protest, but she seemed frozen. I had the sense Hugo was forcing her to say something she otherwise would not have.

"I only meant to put a small hole in her hose, so that she would be forced to go to the surface, but then she turned around so fast that my knife cut through the rubber." Her tone came out without emotion, convincing me that Hugo was playing a role here.

The problem was that her story did not match Alex's account, but maybe it didn't matter. Attempted murder was attempted murder.

"That's not exactly what happened, Jodi."

This time Alex's voice came out rather strong. Too bad Genevieve couldn't float upward as that would make this so cool.

"Yes, it was, I swear."

Steve pushed back his chest. "Jodi Coronado, you are under the arrest for the attempted murder of Alexandria Coronado." He then read her her rights.

"Attempted murder?" she asked.

I guess the gig was up.

"Alex, can you please come in here?" Steve asked.

Mr. Coronado lost all color from his face, but Nina looked elated. I expected to see Alex walk out of Steve's office, but she just appeared alongside Hugo a second later.

"Alex? Is that really you?" her husband asked. "You're alive?"

"I'm very much alive. I realize black is not my normal color, but I couldn't show my face until I found out who had tried to kill me."

"How did you survive?" Jodi asked. That question alone would incriminate her.

"I took precautions." Alex turned to Steve. "Get her out of here. The only three people I want to see are my son, Nina, and Dante." She faced her husband. "As for you? Taking my necklace was the last straw. I didn't realize you would stoop that low."

Nina was the first to hug Alex and then came Gustavo. I thought Ricardo Coronado would try to argue with his wife or at least beg her to take him back, but I guess her anger was something he couldn't bear to deal with right now.

I sort of felt as if I was intruding. Not only that, I didn't like confrontation. "Iggy, we need to go home. And ladies, I couldn't have done this without you."

"I think the credit goes to Genevieve."

I looked around. "Where is she?"

"Probably back at the shop," Andorra said.

Hugo was standing next to Alex. "I'm surprised Hugo's sudden appearance didn't cause the questions to fly," I whispered.

Andorra smiled. "I think they have other things to distract them."

Like Alex's presence. "You are so right."

I gathered the candles, and as I stepped from the room, Jaxson was leaving Steve's office with Nash who was probably preparing to book Jodi for attempted murder. I wanted to believe that it was her love for her husband that made her do it. Hopefully, she just wanted to make the path to corporate success an easier one for Gustavo.

I met up with Jaxson. "Good job, pink lady. You got the killer."

"Attempted killer."

"I stand corrected. Since it's a little early for dinner, what's your pleasure?"

"If you have to ask, then you don't know me very well." I winked just like he had.

"Gross," Iggy said.

I was glad he caught on. "I need to pick up some things at the office first. Plus, we'll have to wait for Alex to stop by to gather her things before we can go back to my place. I really need to shower and change."

"No problem," Jaxson said. "I imagine that Rihanna will be moving back in today, too."

"For sure."

We were halfway up the stairs when something large and furry flew out of the cat door—and it wasn't a cat.

Iggy jumped out of my hands and scurried up my shoulder. "It's a rat. Where's Tippy when I need him?"

As horrified as I was that a rat had been in our office, Iggy's reaction made me laugh. Ah, yes, life in Witch's Cove was never dull.

THE NEXT DAY, I called the exterminator to put out traps should the rat return, and I made sure that Iggy watched closely where they were, so he didn't accidentally get caught in one.

"I'm going to find Tippy," Iggy said.

"Why?" He couldn't stand that seagull.

"I need to let him know that he and his friends have to up

their game. We can't have the rats taking over our beaches."

Poor Iggy. "I don't think Tippy will understand you. It's not like he speaks English."

"I'll find a way. I'll draw a picture if I need to."

Before I could respond, he shot out through the cat door. I bet he wasn't even at the bottom before Alex showed up.

"I'm returning to Atlanta, Glinda, but I wanted to thank you, Jaxson, Rihanna, and everyone else. I couldn't have done this without you. The Pink Iguana Sleuths can expect a little something in the mail."

"You don't have to do that."

"Nonsense. I can afford it, and by the looks of this office, you could stand to do a little redecorating."

I had to laugh. She was right. If nothing else, we could use more seating.

I hugged her goodbye. "How is Gustavo holding up?"

"I think in his heart, he knew Jodi was becoming unhinged. The next few months will be hard, but we'll survive. I will definitely do the merger, but I will recommend that Gustavo take a more active role if he chooses."

"I hope it all works out," I said.

"Me too."

Alex hugged us goodbye and then left. I faced Jaxson. "I could really use a chocolate shake. Care to join me?"

"Always."

I smiled. Finishing a case was the best feeling in the world.

What's next? It's Halloween and spooky things are happening—especially in the cemetery. Check out The Case of The Stolen Pink Tombstone.

Buy on Amazon or read for FREE on Kindle Unlimited

Don't forget to sign up for my Cozy Mystery newsletter *to learn about my discounts and upcoming releases. If you prefer to only receive notices regarding my releases, follow me on BookBub.*
http://smarturl.it/VellaDayNL
bookbub.com/authors/vella-day

> Here is a sneak peak of book 16:
> The Case of The Stolen Pink Tombstone

I'D JUST SAT down on the sofa when Penny Carsted, my best friend, breezed in through the office door, carrying a bottle of wine. Not that Penny didn't often arrive with a gift when we had our girls' night, but she certainly didn't come to the office with wine at three thirty in the afternoon.

Adding to the strangeness was that she'd come from her waitressing job. How could I tell? Penny was still wearing her uniform, which was a skirt covered in pennies. Why pennies? Because my Aunt Fern, who owned the Tiki Hut Grill, required every staff member to wear a costume. I know this, because I used to work there before starting up the Pink Iguana Sleuths with my now fiancé, Jaxson Harrison. Back then, I wore a pink Glinda the Good Witch outfit—but that's a story for another time.

"This is a nice surprise," I said.

She grinned. "I come bearing gifts."

"I can see that." I had no idea what the occasion was. "Have a seat and tell me what's going on." My mouth dropped open when a possibility struck. "You and Hunter got engaged."

She waved her free hand and sat down next to me. "No. We're not like you and Jaxson. We need more time. Besides, I have Tommy to think about. I don't want to confuse him by having his dad there part time and also have it be official between me and Hunter."

"I can understand that." Tommy was her nine-year old son. I nodded to the wine bottle in her hand. "So what is the occasion?"

"I need a favor."

I chuckled. "You didn't need to give me a gift for that. Or do you need the Pink Iguana Sleuths' talents to solve some crime?"

She laughed. "It's nothing like that. Today, I got a call from Tommy's school."

That usually wasn't good. I sobered. "Did something happen?"

"Not exactly, other than one of the mothers who promised to help out with the *Halloween Haunted Cemetery* night for the third graders got sick, and I need a replacement."

Uh-oh. I could connect the dots. "You know I love our cemetery, and you thought I'd be the perfect person to chaperone a bunch of kids. Is that it?"

"Yes. We'd have fun, and you'd be great!" Her eyes widened. The huge intake of breath implied she was hoping I'd say yes. The problem was that I never could say no to Penny, and she knew it.

"Why would I be good?" This should be interesting.

"You must have a bunch of spooky tales to tell. After all, your parents run the funeral home."

That had nothing to do with anything, but I didn't need to argue. "When does this event take place?"

"I knew you'd say yes. It's tomorrow night from eight until nine."

Halloween was on Sunday. "The administration picked Friday because the kids don't have school the next day?"

"Exactly. So, you'll do it?"

"Of course, and I'll even see if I can drag Jaxson with me."

"That's even better. Hunter said he'd try to make it if he can get out of going to some meeting."

On a Friday night? It was possible roaming around a cemetery might not be his thing.

"Perfect. The men can hang out and keep us safe while we try to maintain some control over the kiddies." A very bizarre image crossed my mind. "You know, since Hunter is a wolf shifter, he could roam the cemetery in his animal form and really scare the kids."

Yes, I was kidding, but it would have been fun to see the children's reaction.

"Aren't you the funny one. First of all, Hunter would never do that, and secondly, the kids are nine-years-old. I don't want them scarred for life." She leaned forward. "One of the parents agreed to dress up in a sheet and pretend to be a ghost. That's about as far as I'm willing to take it."

I chuckled. "I thought you didn't want to traumatize the poor kids."

She waved a hand. "If anyone cries, I'll tell them the

truth."

Not only did I love old cemeteries, my nineteen-year old cousin who was in school studying photography loved Hamilton Cemetery even more. "Maybe I can ask Rihanna to come along. She loves going there. I don't know if she's been at night, but whether she has or hasn't, she might want to take pictures, assuming there is enough light."

"Hunter and I were able to check it out last week. They have lights randomly placed throughout the grounds, I guess to prevent people from tripping over any tombstones."

"That makes sense, but I thought they were closed at night."

"Oh yeah, they are, so I'm not sure why they'd need lights." She waved a hand. "All I know, is that the cemetery will be open until nine for the next few days in honor of Halloween."

"Good to know." I stood. "Let me get a bottle opener and some glasses so we can celebrate properly."

"You don't have to drink this now, you know."

I rarely drank, and I certainly didn't drink during the day, but what the heck. "Why not? I have nothing to do. Jaxson is working on the monkey bridge, and we have no cases. We'll stick to one glass."

She giggled. "Drinking in the afternoon is decadent."

"It is. To limit the effects, let me find something to snack on."

I stepped into the makeshift kitchen and grabbed two wine glasses and a corkscrew, along with a bag of cookies. No sooner had I set them on the coffee table when Jaxson returned carrying Iggy.

"How did it go with supervising the installation of the monkey bridge?" I know we had no monkeys in Witch's Cove, Florida, but we had squirrels, cats, maybe some rats, and definitely one very determine iguana who wanted to cross the busy main street while staying out of harm's way.

"Great," Jaxson said.

"It's awesome," my nine-pound pink iguana chimed in.

"What exactly is a monkey bridge and where is it going to be?" Penny asked.

"I'll let Jaxson give you the lowdown since he and Iggy were instrumental in getting it set up. Jaxson, while you give Penny the details, do you mind opening the bottle for us while I grab you a glass?"

"Certainly. What are you celebrating?"

"I'll tell you after you give us the details of Iggy's big adventure."

While he opened the wine, I rushed into the kitchen. As I was retrieving a wine glass for him, Jaxson explained what a monkey bridge was to Penny. We needed to celebrate the long-awaited bridge that would allow Iggy to go from our office to the row of buildings on the other side. His best friend—a mute gargoyle shifter—mostly resided in the Hex and Bones Apothecary, which was where I purchased the ingredients for any spells I did. And yes, I am a witch, which is why I have a familiar—a very chatty talking pink iguana.

When I returned, Jaxson poured us each a small glass.

"Can I have a taste?" Iggy asked.

"Of wine? No. You're too young. Plus, I don't think you'd like wine."

"Let me decide for myself."

"Ask me again in a few years."

"You're no fun."

Maybe not, but I was trying to be a responsible parent. Someday, Jaxson and I would have human children to raise.

I lifted my glass. "To allowing Iggy to safely cross the street."

"It's not finished yet." Iggy dropped down onto his stomach.

I looked over at Jaxson. "When will it be done?"

"Either later today or by tomorrow morning. Just in time for Iggy to watch all of the Halloween festivities from his sacred little bridge."

I didn't like the idea of him being above the traffic in case the bridge gave way. "Are you sure that little piece of string will hold up?" I'd seen the bridge before it was installed. It was about six inches wide and was made of green mesh. The bridge had sides, preventing Iggy from falling off, but no telling how well it was tied at both ends.

"Don't worry. I don't plan to sit up there," Iggy said. "I'll be a target for you know who."

I chuckled, because Iggy's nemesis was a white seagull who had black tipped wings who he'd dubbed, Tippy. Being a typical seagull, he had a tendency to poop at random—or at not so random—times. "That's smart."

"I promise it won't fall into disrepair. I'll make sure the city maintains it," Jaxson said.

"Thank you." I believed him. He loved Iggy as much as I did. Not only that, we'd donated some money to the city to keep the bridge maintained. I was the only one with an iguana so I doubted anyone but Iggy would use it, unless the other animals figured out its use.

"Tell me what you and Penny are celebrating," Jaxson said.

"I came to bribe Glinda into joining me tomorrow night at the elementary school's *Halloween Haunted Cemetery* walk. At night. Spooky, huh? We'll even have a parent dressed up as a ghost to scare the kids. It will be perfect."

Jaxson looked at me. "You agreed?"

"Sure. It'll be fun to see how the kids react. I know a few ghost stories I could tell."

Jaxson shook his head. "Poor kids."

Iggy crawled up onto the coffee table. "I want to go."

"No. It is at night, and the kids might step on you."

He looked up at Jaxson. "Tell her I'll stay in her purse."

Why didn't he ask me? "What are you afraid of, Iggy? That Tippy will come through that cat door and poop on you if we're not here?"

He scurried off the table so fast, all I saw was a blur. I really hadn't meant to frighten him. Poor guy.

"Glinda," Jaxson said.

"Yes?"

"I'll carry him."

Sometimes it wasn't worth the argument. "That works, too."

Iggy didn't emerge from under the sofa, but that was okay. He needed to come to grips with his fear of seagulls—or rather one particular seagull.

Penny finished her wine and then stood. "I need to go, but how about meeting us at the school at seven forty-five?"

"It's a date."

I hugged her goodbye, and once she left, I turned to Jaxson. "You're okay with this?"

"Of course. Besides, Iggy might have fun, if he doesn't get *scared*." The last word was said much louder than the others.

My familiar finally peeked his head out from under the sofa. "Me? Scared?"

"You do know that seagulls fly at night, don't you?" I wasn't trying to dissuade him, but if he got loose, it could be a problem.

"I'm not dumb. I'll stay in your bag to be safe. I just want to hear the little kids shriek when that parent jumps out at them."

"You do that."

I'd just placed the wine glasses in the sink when Rihanna came home from junior college.

"You just missed Penny," I said.

"She was here? What did she want?"

I told her about my exciting Friday night. "You're welcome to join us. I thought you might want to take pictures."

"That sounds fabulous. I've been to Hamilton Cemetery tons of times, but only during the day. Tomorrow night, you said?"

"Yes."

"Are you dressing up?"

"I hadn't thought that far. Aunt Fern isn't doing her usual annual event because of what happened last year, so I didn't pick up another costume." I turned to Jaxson. "You up for a little costume shopping?"

"I have nothing to wear, so sure. And since we did just rent out the empty store across the street to a costume shop,

I'm sure I can find something."

"Great!"

"What will you go as?" Rihanna asked.

Last year I went as Supergirl so that Jaxson could be Superman. "I'm not sure. Since it is a cemetery, maybe I should go as the grim reaper."

"That's what I was going to go as," Rihanna said. I couldn't tell if she was disappointed that we would match, or if she was excited we'd be a pair.

"Maybe it would be cool if all three of us went as grim reapers." I sounded like a geek, I know.

She studied me. "Fine, as long as you wear a pink ribbon on your chest."

"Why? Because I always wear pink?" Or almost always.

She rolled her eyes like only a teenager could do. "The pink means that you get to take the souls of the pure people."

I laughed. "You made that up."

"Okay, maybe I did."

I looked up at Jaxson. "You good with this?"

"Anything for you, but I can't imagine there will be a lot of costumes left in the store. Halloween is in three days."

He usually wasn't this pessimistic. "We won't know unless we ask. Besides, I imagine Mr. Mortimer will be happy to have the business."

Jaxson nodded to Iggy. "What about smaller sizes?"

"He can wear his Tippy-proof cape."

My Aunt Fern had recently made him one to protect him when Iggy went outside. This panicked request by my familiar happened after one of the local seagulls began tormenting poor Iggy. Of late, he hadn't been wearing it, but he still had it.

"Sounds good. Want to check it out now?" Jaxson said.

I looked over at Rihanna whose closet was comprised of mostly black clothes. She didn't need to buy a grim reaper outfit. "Care to join us?"

"Sure, I'd love to see what this new place carries."

"Me, too." Even though Jaxson and I had purchased the strip of stores across the street after receiving a windfall from our most bizarre case, Jaxson and our lawyers had done the transaction with Mr. Mortimer. I'd yet to meet the owner.

Buy On Amazon

THE END

A WITCH'S COVE MYSTERY (Paranormal Cozy Mystery)
PINK Is The New Black (book 1)
A PINK Potion Gone Wrong (book 2)
The Mystery of the PINK Aura (book 3)
Box Set (books 1-3)
Sleuthing In The PINK (book 4)
Not in The PINK (book 5)
Gone in the PINK of an Eye (book 6)
Box Set (books 4-6)
The PINK Pumpkin Party (book 7)
Mistletoe with a PINK Bow (book 8)
The Magical PINK Pendant (book 9)
The Poisoned PINK Punch (book 10)
PINK Smoke and Mirrors (book 11)
Broomsticks and PINK Gumdrops (book 12)
Knotted Up In PINK Yarn (book 13)
Ghosts and PINK Candles (book 14)
Pilfered PINK Pearls (book 15)
The Case of the Stolen PINK Tombstone (book 16)
The PINK Christmas Cookie Caper (book 17)
Pink Moon Rising (book 18)

SILVER LAKE SERIES (3 OF THEM)
(1). HIDDEN REALMS OF SILVER LAKE (Paranormal Romance)
Awakened By Flames (book 1)
Seduced By Flames (book 2)
Kissed By Flames (book 3)
Destiny In Flames (book 4)
Box Set (books 1-4)

Passionate Flames (book 5)
Ignited By Flames (book 6)
Touched By Flames (book 7)
Box Set (books 5-7)
Bound By Flames (book 8)
Fueled By Flames (book 9)
Scorched By Flames (book 10)

(2). **FOUR SISTERS OF FATE: HIDDEN REALMS OF SILVER LAKE** (Paranormal Romance)
Poppy (book 1)
Primrose (book 2)
Acacia (book 3)
Magnolia (book 4)
Box Set (books 1-4)
Jace (book 5)
Tanner (book 6)

(3). **WERES AND WITCHES OF SILVER LAKE**
(Paranormal Romance)
A Magical Shift (book 1)
Catching Her Bear (book 2)
Surge of Magic (book 3)
The Bear's Forbidden Wolf (book 4)
Her Reluctant Bear (book 5)
Freeing His Tiger (book 6)
Protecting His Wolf (book 7)
Waking His Bear (book 8)
Melting Her Wolf's Heart (book 9)
Her Wolf's Guarded Heart (book 10)
His Rogue Bear (book 11)

Box Set (books 1-4)
Box Set (books 5-8)
Reawakening Their Bears (book 12)

OTHER PARANORMAL SERIES
PACK WARS (Paranormal Romance)
Training Their Mate (book 1)
Claiming Their Mate (book 2)
Rescuing Their Virgin Mate (book 3)
Box Set (books 1-3)
Loving Their Vixen Mate (book 4)
Fighting For Their Mate (book 5)
Enticing Their Mate (book 6)
Box Set (books 1-4)
Complete Box Set (books 1-6)

HIDDEN HILLS SHIFTERS (Paranormal Romance)
An Unexpected Diversion (book 1)
Bare Instincts (book 2)
Shifting Destinies (book 3)
Embracing Fate (book 4)
Promises Unbroken (book 5)
Bare 'N Dirty (book 6)
Hidden Hills Shifters Complete Box Set (books 1-6)

CONTEMPORARY SERIES
MONTANA PROMISES (Full length contemporary Romance)
Promises of Mercy (book 1)
Foundations For Three (book 2)
Montana Fire (book 3)

Montana Promises Box Set (books 1-3)
Hart To Hart (Book 4)
Burning Seduction (Book 5)
Montana Promises Complete Box Set (books 1-5)

ROCK HARD, MONTANA (contemporary romance novellas)
Montana Desire (book 1)
Awakening Passions (book 2)

PLEDGED TO PROTECT (contemporary romantic suspense)
From Panic To Passion (book 1)
From Danger To Desire (book 2)
From Terror To Temptation (book 3)
Pledged To Protect Box Set (books 1-3)

BURIED SERIES (contemporary romantic suspense)
Buried Alive (book 1)
Buried Secrets (book 2)
Buried Deep (book 3)
The Buried Series Complete Box Set (books 1-3)

A NASH MYSTERY (Contemporary Romance)
Sidearms and Silk(book 1)
Black Ops and Lingerie(book 2)
A Nash Mystery Box Set (books 1-2)

STARTER SETS (Romance)
Contemporary
Paranormal

Author Bio

Love it HOT and STEAMY? Sign up for my newsletter and receive MONTANA DESIRE for FREE. smarturl.it/o4cz93?IQid=MLite

OR Are you a fan of quirky PARANORMAL COZY MYSTERIES? Sign up for this newsletter. smarturl.it/CozyNL

Not only do I love to read, write, and dream, I'm an extrovert. I enjoy being around people and am always trying to understand what makes them tick. Not only must my romance books have a happily ever after, I need characters I can relate to. My men are wonderful, dynamic, smart, strong, and the best lovers in the world (of course).

My Paranormal Cozy Mysteries are where I let my imagination run wild with witches and a talking pink iguana who believes he's a real sleuth.

I believe I am the luckiest woman. I do what I love and I have a wonderful, supportive husband, who happens to be hot!

Fun facts about me

(1) I'm a math nerd who loves spreadsheets. Give me numbers and I'll find a pattern.

(2) I live on a Costa Rica beach!

(3) I also like to exercise. Yes, I know I'm odd.

I love hearing from readers either on FB or via email (hint, hint).

Social Media Sites

Website: www.velladay.com
FB: facebook.com/vella.day.90
Twitter: @velladay4
Gmail: velladayauthor@gmail.com

Printed in Great Britain
by Amazon